The Graveyard Shift: Aftermath

S. Hodgson

Copyright ©2010 Simon Hodgson All rights reserved.
No part of this book may be reproduced in any form without
written permission from the publisher.
ISBN: 978-1-4457-2285-6

The Graveyard Shift: Aftermath

By Simon Hodgson

Chapter 1

The day had started the same as the last three, it was two hours until midday and the sun was shining brightly in the clear blue sky. In quite a contradiction to the normal April showers it had been a long time since the last raindrops had fallen to earth and the weather appeared once more that it would be glorious, tainted only by the slightest cold breeze. This should have been nothing but a pleasantry for Matthew Hughes but it was far from that. He was grateful of course for this slight joy, he hated being wet and cold but he still found it hard to get excited or happy about anything now especially something like the British weather actually being nice for a change.

He tried to look around at the cloudless heavens and absorb the fact that it was very warm and indeed pleasant for an English spring but no joy arose within him and it didn't take much of his brain power to figure out why he felt so empty inside. Each day that came and went now was always the same, it wouldn't matter if the sun melted or if it were to start raining bars of gold, nothing would evoke emotion or change the thing that ate away at him constantly. It was that fucking noise! Not the fear that related to the deafening sound but just that constant thrum of groaning and wailing that never ever stopped. It was tearing and shredding away at his self-resistance every minute of every god forsaken day and he knew that it would be like that probably for as long as he was going to live, however long that may be. It didn't matter how many doors he barricaded himself behind or how loud he tried to make his thoughts that sound just never fucking disappeared, if anything it seemed to grow even louder with each passing minute.

It wasn't just like that for him though, the two people he was holed up with had to endure the same torment and it seemed that it was affecting them too albeit in various manners. To be fair though no fucker could make it through what was happening and remain mentally unscathed, it was simply impossible.

The three of them had already accomplished so much by staying alive this far but Matt took little comfort in that fact, he was beginning to wonder what the point in running and fighting was for when the road ahead looked just as bad as what they had already had to deal with. It was hard to remain positive when it seemed that there would be no end to the misery although he did know deep down that he was so very lucky to still be alive and should actually cherish every breath of air that he was taking. It was just damn hard considering everything that they had to contend with on a daily basis including the knowledge that they may be the only disease free humans left. He just hoped that his strength didn't get too depleted from this looming fact that was everywhere that they looked. He knew though that regardless of what shit was still to come the three of them had to keep their spirits up as much as possible and so far considering everything that had happened they were doing a pretty damn good job.

Sean Ryes seemed fairly calm making an allowance for the heap of crap that they found themselves in, happily whistling away to himself throughout the days that crawled by and quite often joking about and at least trying to have a laugh at any opportunity that presented itself. Matt was quite sure it was all just a defensive barricade to stop him from cracking but if it worked for the big man then so be it, and it did tend to keep morale as high as possible having someone with a positive attitude about. He was a huge figure of a man which seemed to add a feeling of security to their group, with his size and strength it would take an army of the fuckers to drag him down that was for sure.

Abbey Starks seemed to be holding up like the two men but the strain had begun to tell over the last few days. She had been found crying a few times now, looking at the pendant she carried with her that contained the photos of her husband and child, both of whom had long since been swallowed up by this fucked up mess that surrounded them. That was as much as the two men knew though, she had not been willing to part with any more information than that but they were also not willing to pry. After all any loss especially one so close was hard enough to deal with and facing a million questions would hardly help the situation.

Poor bitch probably hadn't even had the chance to grieve for them either. She was fucking strong though of that Matt had no doubt, she had after all survived three months in this nightmare which was more than most of the population had managed so she certainly had it in her to shake of this bout of sadness that had recently crept up and grabbed her tightly. Besides all three of them had by now faced the facts that everyone that they had known, loved or cared for were most probably dead. Actually there was no probably about it, they were dead, and worst of all they had most probably been eaten or had become part of the contaminated army of the dead that covered everything around them.

It was as Matt took a long look at those beautiful red rimmed blue eyes of Abbey's that he heard and almost felt Sean's deep bellowing voice shouting the one thing that none of them had wanted to hear.

"They're fucking through!"

The trio of survivors had reached the builder's compound only four days before and with the sight of a six-foot chain link fence surrounding it, the place had looked like a paradise to them. Finding somewhere secure and uninfected had become like searching for the Holy Grail, those fuckers were everywhere and that made the task a million times more challenging and dangerous. Unfortunately this duty of finding a safe haven had become the one necessity of their lives now, which meant that once they discovered a safe place they wanted to stay put. Once inside the compound, they had hoped to hide out for at least a week or two before continuing on their journey to try and find other survivors, food, drink and possibly even help but once again life seemed unwilling to throw them a bone. They had carried out parameter checks, strengthened the fence as best they could with the limited supplies they had and even found some rations to help them last a little longer but those things just kept on coming and pressing their weight against the outside of the mesh barrier wanting just one thing which was access to the three people within. They had known that it wouldn't hold up forever but the fact that it had only lasted this long was yet another low blow that they had to face and now had to deal with.

After hearing the large man's voice, Matthew and Abbey sprang to their feet and readied their weapons whilst retreating hastily towards an open sewer lid about fifty yards behind them. The creatures seemed to be pouring through the newly created gap in the fence, the stinking, rotting figures moving as fast as their decaying corpses would allow as they tried to reach the back pedalling threesome. Thankfully for them the sewer entrance was an escape route that had been pre-planned on their arrival, as they had known that the time to flee would come sooner or later it had been a better safe than sorry idea. It was the same way that they had reached the compound leaving them with the knowledge that it was zombie free. At least it was the perfect way for them to escape albeit back to the murky depths below which in the grand scheme of things were still better than remaining on the surface to be eaten.

After retreating quickly, it was only a few moments until Matt and Abbey caught up with Sean who had already begun firing his Beretta into the slowly approaching crowd of monsters whilst preparing for the descent down below.

"Fuck!" Were the only words that left Matt's mouth as they reached the escape hatch from which the unmistakeable smell of human waste rose, it seemed that they must begin yet another search for refuge if indeed there was anywhere left for them to hide. With their continuing travels it seemed there were less and less suitable places for them to shelter, he just hoped that they managed to find somewhere else soon.

As they climbed down the ladder into the murky gloom, Abbey first followed by Matt and then Sean the grinding sound of the metal lid being slid back into its opening bounced off the tunnel walls around them. Matt smiled momentarily as the light from above eclipsed and the darkness enveloped him; he realized that the loudness of the grate had almost for a second drowned out the sounds of death that he had grown so used to. He couldn't help but wonder if the moment that had just passed in the blink of an eye was the closest he would ever come to peace and quiet again, but unfortunately he knew he didn't have any time to even dwell on that thought and so with this he made his way down into the sewers.

As Abbey illuminated a large torch and the three of them gathered their thoughts for a second they knew there was only one way to go. This was the same tunnel that had led them to the builder's yard so it was a simple matter of heading in the same direction that they had been doing so far, there was nothing behind them but death, destruction and bad memories. Sean took some cigarettes from his pocket, took three from the crumpled pack and passed one to Matt and Abbey before retrieving his lighter and igniting them each in turn. As he returned his hand to his pocket the distinct familiar sounds of scratching began from above them, as the following pack of monstrosities reached the now sealed entrance to the sewers. Matt lowered his head and exhaled heavily as a blue plume of smoke filled the air around him. "Fucking zombies." Were the only words to softly leave his mouth before the three of them began what they knew was going to be a long hard walk.

Chapter 2

The wind blew violently and whistled its eerie tune through the few shards of glass that remained in Frank Garret's full-length kitchen window. He stood panting heavily; beads of sweat were glistening on every inch of his skin while his hands trembled violently by his sides. The battle had lasted only minutes but for the aches and pains he was now feeling he could have sworn he had just run five marathons back to back, either that or been hit repeatedly by Mike Tyson. He didn't look any better than he felt either, blood and gore staining almost every inch of him, the sight making his skin itch through the un-cleanliness that he suddenly felt.
The bastards hadn't really been that strong but their clumsiness made them almost impossible to deal with, especially when three of them had managed to break their way through in one swift go. Luckily Frank had managed to arm himself with many makeshift weapons since the mayhem had first begun, most of which he had retrieved from within his garden shed on the day that the incident reports began. He had always lived his life by being quite overcautious but for once this approach had not only paid off but also saved his life on numerous occasions so far. Most people had taken it as a joke when the reports of zombies had started on the news and radio but thankfully he had not, which he knew was one of the main reasons he was still breathing.

Out of all the supplies he had, his spade had proven so far more useful than he had ever thought possible especially in the fight that had just occurred. Held widthways across his body it had made the perfect barrier to hold away the biting jaws as two of the creatures had managed to grab him and wrestle him to the ground. It had taken an almighty effort to push them off within the narrow room before the young man had regained his footing and took hold of the situation using his pure animal instinct and the anger that was raging within. Having just enough room to swing the digging tool he had decapitated the first two that had broken through and grabbed him before spearing the third through the stomach. The implement slid easily through the dead grey fleshy midriff, the only slight resistance coming from the creature's spine, which snapped clean through from the brute force of the blow. Frank hated the fact that practically nothing stopped these fucking abominations and just watching the twitching figure on the ground beneath his feet made the bile rise to the back of his throat.

Seeing the two heads that had bounced across his slate tiled floor and the bodies that they had once been apart of he struggled to accept that he had actually just beheaded two people, it was just so fucked up it couldn't be real. Something so bizarre would probably never fully sink in to any ones system but despite his efforts to deal with it, he still found everything around him such an impossible effort to swallow. How could you fucking accept that despite the fact that the last creature had been almost cut in half and had a broken back, the monster in his kitchen was still trying with what mobility it had to reach him and devour his flesh. If he ever made it through this he would need a shit load of counselling and prescription drugs of that he was certain but the simple thought of there ever being an end to this mess looked very unlikely in the first place.

Thankfully though, this fight at least for now was over and Garred was almost grateful that he had to make a new barricade for the back window, it would surely only be minutes before more of them things found their way into his back garden in the search of warm human meat so he did not have long to accomplish this task. First though he would have to move the three stricken creatures out of his house, despite two now being officially dead, whatever that meant and one being pretty much disabled and harmless the smell was enough to make him dispose of them rather than to leave them be. It was as he rubbed a drip of sweat from his eyebrow that a groan came sailing in with the wind through the gaping hole that had once been his double-glazed window. He knew that despite his tiredness and lack of energy he had to get moving and get these monsters back outside; time was once again of the essence, as it always seemed to be with everything that he did now.

At twenty-five years old Garred was in the prime of his life and up until the world seemed to fall on its arse a few months before, he had loved every aspect of his existence. He was a handsome young man who had a very likeable personality and each day he always seemed to wake with a spring in his step.

  He had been promoted to head of his sales department at the sorting office where he worked a nine to five week and had managed to scoop player of the year for his Sunday league football team all in the space of the last six months. On top of this, he lived in a nice house in a nice area, had some great friends and family so everything had been looking like sunshine until of course the disaster began to destroy everything around him. He had lived on his own in what he liked to call his bachelor pad for two years, although the fact that he had recently settled down and his girlfriend of three months had just moved in kind of eradicated that view although this fact had once again changed over the past few days. Sharon, who he classed as the love of his life already after such a short space of time was everything he could have ever wished for in a partner, they shared a love for all of the same things, they loved each other's company, shared each other's passions and on top of that she was his best friend from whom he hid nothing.

But as suddenly as she had come into his life, they had taken this wonderful relationship away from him. Those fucking zombies had managed to break through the front door barricade while the two of them had slept and grabbed her, one fucking bite to the neck and she was done, snatched from his life as simple as that, leaving him to watch the nightmare unfold in front of his very eyes. There was nothing he could have done, by the time he had snapped awake from his slumber she was already done for although that didn't stop him from trying to rescue her as he heard her terrified screams ringing out through the house. By the time he got to her though she had been dragged half way through the opening and her eyes had become glazed and lifeless, had he gone any further he would have been taken too leaving him with only one option which was to push the fuckers back out and barricade himself inside once again. It was so unfair, they had battled side by side, surviving for so long together through the horror in their home and dealing with everything that these bastards could throw at them except for one attack and one loose barricade which had proven so bloody costly. Christ they had even managed missions outside amongst the hordes to stock up on food from deserted neighbourhood houses without getting bitten but this had cost him everything. How he wanted her back so badly, he missed her and even though she had only been gone two weeks he felt so alone and lost without her.

    He was now completely unaided in this mess and it seemed to be getting no easier as the time went by. He knew of course that he had to battle on but the future looked so bleak without Sharon in it, all the strength that she gave him was now gone and the fact that these fuckers had done this, it had only served to replace his strength with a boiling rage that he struggled to control. He knew that acting on anger could make him careless but Frank accepted there was nothing he could really do about that fact. Nothing could get rid of the fury that he felt for those stumbling corpses outside, it wasn't simply something that he could forget or just push to the back of his mind, it was a permanent fixture within now. He would just carry on fighting for his continuation and just hope that somehow he came out the other side of this although since his loved ones demise the doubts were quickly rising and his constant questioning of what he had to live for only depleted his morale even more.

    Grabbing the two severed heads first, Frank made his way towards the kitchen door that led into his back garden, given the choice he would have much rather stayed inside but he just couldn't stomach having those things indoors with him regardless of how harmless they now were. He pushed the handle down with his elbow and used his knee to open the door catching a fierce blast of wind in his face as he did so. The warmth of the day had now receded only to be replaced with the type of weather that should usually be expected during the spring season. The wind and cold its self bothered Frank little but he knew because of the elements he would have to remain more aware than ever should any noises go unheard thanks to the newly raging conditions. He edged out a foot or so looking around the lawn until satisfied it was clear before hurling the two skulls into the hedge about six foot or so away from him.

"Let the fucking foxes have you!" He said out loud with venom regretting that he had done so immediately in case any unwanted attention would be alerted from his bellowing comment. Feeling something moist on his hands he looked down horrified to notice that some of the dead flesh and matted hair from one of the skulls had clung to his grip. He shook his hand frantically with disgust, immediately happy once the slice of rotting scalp hit the floor with a slap. He exhaled partially through disgust and partly from tiredness before he heard the wailing once again from down the side of the house, the noise causing the hairs on his neck to stand to attention. He took a few steps and peered down the alleyway to see that the gate that he hoped would remain closed had in fact been opened slightly which explained the three corpses that had come crashing through his kitchen window.

Thankfully his rubbish bin was stopping it from opening fully which was hindering the newly arrived groaning creatures progress round back. This particular zombie had obviously been a woman who in life had been very fond of her food; she was monumental to say the least and this was the simple reason why unlike the three zombies before her she couldn't get through the tight gap.

One of her arms was missing and it seemed one of her knees had been twisted almost backwards but she somehow managed to keep her huge frame upright despite these horrific injuries that in life surely would have left her grounded.

Thankfully though after watching her for almost a full minute Garred was more than satisfied that she wasn't coming through at any point in the near future leaving him enough time to complete his task of corpse removal without the worry of another unexpected attack. One by one he dragged the cold clammy bodies out into his garden and as far away from the house as possible, ensuring though that he kept a good guard all the way through and trying as much as he could to look away from the one creature that still lived. It took him just over five minutes and a lot of energy he didn't have but Frank got the job done and was happy to hear the kitchen door close behind him once again. Once the key had been turned, he slid down the inside of the door and felt a trickle of water run down his cheek. He was so emotional he honestly couldn't tell if it was sweat or a tear but when more followed he knew it was the latter. It was the first time since everything had occurred that he had let any form of emotion show and he wasn't surprised that it had finally come, after all he had watched his partner die only two weeks before and he was fucking exhausted. It wasn't that he had fought against his emotions he just hadn't had any time to even think about them, every minute had been spent keeping the house secure and ensuring that he remained safe. He allowed himself a couple of minutes to get out the grief that had been hiding while taking a few hefty swallows from his Jack Daniels that had fallen to the floor during the attack, he needed a fucking drink and he needed some rest more than he had ever needed it in his life.

He was shivering and as his eyes swam into focus it took a moment for Frank to realise that he was facing the silver bin in his kitchen rather than the wall like he remembered. The moisture on his groin and the toppled bottle of bourbon explained themselves but a look at the glowing clock hands immediately struck fear into his very soul. He didn't need to tell himself that he had fallen asleep while the window next to him was gaping wide and he had been out of it for nearly four hours, how the hell he hadn't woken to find a zombie attached to his jugular was beyond him. He couldn't give a shit that he had spilled nearly a litre of whiskey of which he only had two bottles left but he had let his guard down in a really big way, which he knew he couldn't afford. Christ he should have been zombie food.

It was pitch black outside and so cold compared to the few nights before but more than that he knew how lucky he was that he hadn't been eaten. It took him and his sleepy legs a few seconds to stand up before he flicked on the torch and shone it outside, both thankful and surprised to see there were none of the zombies waiting for him, presumably the fat one had blocked the way for any other monsters but it mattered little, he had been fucking lucky, end of story. The tools that Frank needed for making another barrier for the window had already been gathered at the same time he had stocked up on his makeshift weapons so luckily the job of making another blockade was no huge task. Part of his garden fence had paid the toll for the supplies he had taken but he knew that it was a small price to pay for him to try and make the house secure against these fucking zombies. It was with another weary exhale that Frank picked up the first panel of wood and a hammer, it was so hard for him to get motivated but after what he had seen there was no way he would let those bastards take him, he could think of a million other ways he would rather die than to be fucking chewed to death or even worse turn into one of those bastard things.

It was three in the morning before he was happy that his newly made panels would withstand those flesh hungry freaks and it was half an hour later that he once again fell asleep although this time it was in the comfort of his living room chair with a half drunken glass of whiskey in his hand. He could no longer keep his body going and had given in to the fight against slumber and once again against his pent up emotions as he had dozed off with the tears still leaking from his reddened eyes.

Chapter 3

"Hey, that one looks familiar." Were Sean's comments as he tried to amuse himself and cheer up the other two as he often found himself doing. As the large chunk of excrement floated by his leg, he had noticed that the conversation from his two companions had dropped to a non-existent level during the past hours worth of hiking which was something that he didn't want to happen. It was hard enough to walk around in a dark, wet, shit filled tunnel as it was but to do it in complete silence made things a damn sight worse, besides he had always been the talkative type and he was hardly about to let an apocalypse stop that. The quietness of the tunnels gave them all too much time to ponder the fucked up nature of everything that had happened which was the main reason behind the current silence. It was this that had made Sean adopt his usual upbeat manner to get them chatting once again.

They had been walking for a long time now and the going was getting much worse which was another thing that they could have done without. The shit filled water was now thigh deep and seeming to grow thicker, the smell simply beyond comprehension. It was unlike anything any of them had ever imagined and it didn't seem that it would get any easier as they moved on with each laboured step wondering whether the stench of death above would be a nicer intrusion. It had also been a while since they had passed an overhead grate for them to look out of which had begun to raise a few concerns on their whereabouts, even though most of the glances at street level revealed nothing but zombies it was at least a break from the constant walking and gave them a short opportunity to rest.

Although all from Sheffield they had travelled so far now that everything was quite new to them and being underground there was no chance of them even beginning to guess what may lie above, all they knew was that they had been heading south. They assumed that they were still following the same main road as before, the tunnel had remained the same size, which seemed like a good thing but in all reality it told them very little. They could soon reach the bloody coastline as far as any of them were concerned but so long as they found safety it mattered little where they ended up. None of them were trained for this sort of expedition, they simply had their instincts to trust and that was all. The weapons that they now owned had been found on the dead, the survival tactics that they had so far employed had mainly been impulse and it seemed that escaping through the tunnels could turn out to be a bad idea too.

Since the three of them had met in one of West Street's many bars they had accomplished so much to stay alive and in reality through all the horror they had become friends even though the situation had been forced on them. It was the day that the main wrath of the plague tore through Sheffield that they had first crossed paths, the evil began infecting everyone around them at such a pace that all that could be done was to hide and hope. It had been late on a Saturday evening when the shit had hit the fan resulting in the three strangers taking refuge in the same bar together. To begin with there was a group of maybe twenty-five people inside with them however this number did not last long. Some were already bitten, carriers waiting to die and then come back as one of them, others snapped under the pressure of knowing their loved ones may be dead and ventured outside soon to be torn to pieces and devoured.

Not a day went by without someone dying until three remained, Matt, Sean and Abbey were all that had survived the terror but they too had to finally up and leave the delicate safety of the bar. They had possessed no food and no weapons meaning that they had simply faced no other choice apart from to stay there and starve to death. That had been over two months ago now although it seemed more like years for all that they had fought through since that last day in the pub. Since then they had all acquired weapons, supplies and they had all certainly turned from the civilised people they once were into toughened shells just prepared to fight for their lives each and every day. Unfortunately though the fight still seemed never ending and they knew that it actually could be a battle that would never be won, as far as they were concerned they could be the last people alive but it was certainly not worth giving up, nothing was worse than the prospect of becoming one of them. They would simply have to hope that as they moved on, more supplies and weapons could be found and eventually the bliss of a rescue or at least an uninfected area.

As the trio rounded another bend in the sewer pipe Abbey and Sean stopped immediately with their jaws hanging agape. Matthew who had been looking into the water carried on walking unaware to the sight ahead of him until he felt a cool breeze on his damp clothing and his sweat stained brow. It was only then that he realised the other two had stopped moving and that he had been pretty fucking blind to miss the bizarre scene that presented its self ahead. About five hundred yards or so in front of where Matt Hughes now stood the pipe in which they were yawned wide open revealing the street and sky above. Luckily only one of the zombies had fallen through the cavern and looking at the way it splashed about and struggled to stay above the water the fucker had pleasantly broken both its legs on the way down.

Disgustingly the water seemed to be helping to make this thing more grotesque, bits of its sagging rotten flesh peeling off into the dark murky liquid as it tried to groan through its water filled lungs, only managing to release a throaty gargle with each attempt as its head bobbed about on the surface. It was pretty impossible to tell if this creature had been man or woman in life but it didn't bear thinking about when dealing with them, any sign of emotion or thought could cost you your life, which is why as Abbey walked past Matt and began to approach the scene she pulled the knife from her belt and slid it expressionlessly into the skull of the floundering zombie pinning it to the wall of the tunnel.

Although she knew it wouldn't terminate the demon she knew it would keep the fucking thing out of the way and allow them all to pass safely without having to worry about being bitten. They had learned by now that to kill these things you had to completely destroy or remove the head but that was a lot of work and effort that usually hindered rather than helped them. Beheading someone rather than just putting a bullet into their skull was too fucking time consuming that was for sure as they had found out on a few occasions throughout their travels. For now though Abbey was happy to leave behind one of the three knives she was carrying to immobilise the creature so that they could properly assess the situation at hand. After all she still had her automatic pistol too so at the minute she had sufficient weaponry to see her through although none of them knew what was lying in wait above on street level. The only thing that was immediately apparent was that up was the only option as the tunnel had been completely blocked making their continued journey underground impossible.

As the two men joined Abbey only feet from the blackened carnage it was not hard to tell what had happened but once again it was just another vision that looked so surreal to them. Pretty much most things they saw now were nightmarish and mind boggling just adding to the library of fucked up images that were being stored in their brains and this new one would be another unwelcome addition. A small jet had obviously plummeted to the ground or attempted a landing and come straight through the fucking road which now lay in ruins right before their eyes. It had probably run out of fuel waiting for a response from a nearby airport, which had never come although there were many reasons that the trio could have pondered behind this devastating accident.

Burned and obliterated bodies were fucking everywhere and it was impossible to tell how many deceased there were scattered all over the place. The fire had long since burned its self out but looking at the charred carnage it had been raging when the incident had actually happened. Most of the human remains had been scorched through to the bone and sickeningly there was still the sweet smell of cooked flesh lingering in the tunnel, so much so that Sean covered his face to try and rid his nostrils of the faint stench. The smell of zombies and shit filled sewers was one thing that he had grown to almost tolerate but the smell of barbequed skin was too much for him to take as he felt his stomach doing somersaults.

As Abbey looked at the metal remains of the aircraft that were twisted and warped from the intense heat that they had been in contact with she noticed they were coloured black like everything else that had been involved. Abbey took the first step forward, pressing her foot on to what had been part of the wing to test out its stability. It bounced slightly but thankfully as the young woman had hoped, it was wedged in pretty tight and would lead them upwards to the street. The movements in the water that had been caused by her action stirred up a few hidden body parts that had been caused by the crash. Horrifyingly some of the limbs that appeared in the brown cloudy water had been those belonging to children killed in the crash, the tiny broken and burned pieces floating lifelessly on the surface, an instant reminder of how brutally cruel this fucked up mess was and the horrifying fact that no one was safe from it either.

The urge to return to the top and get away from the carnage was strong within the trio now and it was Abbey that once again took the lead beginning a steady and cautious climb up the wreckage. It felt nice as the fresh air invaded her nostrils, certainly a welcomed break from the foul stench of a million turds that they had been forced to breathe for the last God knows how long. The sounds of the zombies were as always clear as day but until she climbed level with the street Abbey was unsure how many of the fucking things there would be. She could only hope there would be enough room for them to get by and find some refuge otherwise they were shit out of luck as this was the only way forward that they had. The tunnel was definitely a no go because of the wreck, which left the only option of the street, or a trip back the way they had already come which they all knew would be completely pointless.

As she took another two carefully placed steps Abbey almost smiled as she saw what came into view, sure there were members of the undead spread out all over but that she had expected. The school that was heavily fenced off, she certainly hadn't and from what she could see it looked clear, none of the fuckers seemed to be stumbling about inside the grounds. Going by the minute size of the education centre it was obviously private but the eight-foot high steel bars that surrounded the place would be fucking perfect for the shelter and safety that the group so desperately needed not to mention the fact that the place would probably have a canteen too. "There is a fenced off school we can use," She said without turning round to look at the two men who she knew were right behind her. Matt and Sean were yet to see the street level but taking into account the excitement in her voice their hopes began to rise immediately. Abbey was already looking at the fastest route to cover the two hundred yards to the goal that they needed to reach, thinking of the most foolproof way possible.

Without counting exactly she guessed that there were six of those infected things to get by, the closest of which was a man with a gaping hole where his lungs had once sat in his chest cavity. He had noticed her and had begun a slow clumsy shuffle in her direction but it mattered little, there was a three-foot gap from the road surface to the wing on which she stood. Very little took her by surprise any more but she would be pretty fucking shocked if they had learned how to jump or otherwise navigate their way past a problem like the one that this zombie now faced. She waited another thirty seconds before her thoughts were confirmed and the foul stinking creature plummeted into the water below without having even hesitated to step out into the nothingness between them. These things, as deadly as they were, didn't have any form of fucking intellect that was for sure which made it even harder to believe that they had taken over the whole country or as far as they knew the whole fucking world so damn fast.

The sudden flash of a zombie falling past them made both Sean and Matt jump, at the point where they stood this creature had been out of their sight ensuring that neither man had seen it coming. Neither had time to catch his breath though as Abbey leapt onto the concrete and told them to follow, it seemed that they were heading to this school without discussion although they both trusted her judgement and knew that they faced little other choice being as though a fucking aircraft had blocked their route. They watched as Abbey planted a heavy kick to the knees of the first lunging corpse, its fragile and decayed bones shattering under the blow as it collapsed and hit the ground with a sickening thump and a dull lifeless moan.

The fact that half of this creatures skull was missing made the impact worse as some greyish brain tissue spattered the earth around its stricken body almost hitting the two running men as they sped past careful not to lose their footing on the gooey greyish tissue. Focused on what was ahead though the men continued, following the leaders nimble footsteps as she side stepped three more of the zombies before coming face to face with the last two of them that stood between her and the refuge that they so urgently needed. Sean, seeing her stop immediately stepped past and removed his gun firing off two shots into the face of both creatures knowing that this would ground them and give them chance to get inside.

As he watched them fall, he enjoyed the burning smell of cordite in his nostrils before moving forward to the school gate with a smile on his face, he knew he could have probably saved his ammo and used his boots or even his fists but the rush that it gave him to use the pistol was just too hard to refuse and any excuse to put a hole in any of these bastards was good enough for him. As the big man reached out to the gate, to his shocked delight he found that it was actually unbolted leaving him free to step to one side and allow his two comrades inside into what they hoped would be a new found long term safety for them. Once inside, Matt immediately suggested they should investigate and as Sean bolted the gate behind them an almighty scream erupted from inside the main building in front of which they now stood.

The hairs on the backs of their necks immediately stood up at this sudden intrusion of their senses, they had heard plenty of screams and other noises through all of their battles but this was a sound that had become almost none existent to them all. The scream that they had just heard was from another human being, it seemed that someone else had survived.

Chapter 4

The zombie plague had begun in nearby Chesterfield and had remained largely unseen and unreported by the time it had hit Nottingham, which unfortunately left the large city and its resident's unsuspecting and easy prey. The groaning figures had initially begun working their way through the surrounding villages and towns; spreading terror and pandemonium as they infected all those that they could grab hold of and sink their teeth into, the further that they moved the faster the infection had continued to spread.

Survivors had tried to seek any refuge they could but usually amongst those that actually made it indoors were some who had received infectious wounds. This meant simply that the majority still met their demise regardless of where they hid or how much they had tried to fight for their lives. Those who tried to escape by car were swamped by masses of the undead and it did not take long until the whole city had been overpowered and taken, the residents either turned into monsters or simply eaten alive. The option to flee had simply become impossible amongst the chaos, all routes of escape were simply jammed with bodies, zombies and abandoned vehicles. Despite the lack of skills that these monsters carried the pandemonium and speed with which the plague travelled combined with the complete unawareness of the situation was simply too overpowering for any form of defence to be mounted.

Those few that miraculously lasted beyond the first few days either starved or died trying to escape, finding it impossible to navigate past the masses of dead or the destruction that had occurred everywhere that this plague had touched. Some fires still burned freely as the metropolis that had once been bustling now stood at a complete standstill, the only product of this once thriving place a constant thrum of noise coming from the millions of flesh hungry monsters that now lined every road and pavement still in the eternal search for the warm moist meat that they so craved.

In the centre of Nottingham's shopping district it was pretty much the same as the areas that surrounded it, desolate, destroyed and swarming by those that walked without a heartbeat. The football ground had burned to nothing but a shell and even the arena had been caught up in an explosion that had reduced it to little more than rubble. Nottingham City Theatre that had once been such a proud and monumental building was no different as it stood in complete ruins. The once beautiful and majestic structure was now nothing but an eyesore in the middle of the city, with nothing of its previous glamour left to show.

Half of the building now stood crumbled, burned and collapsed leaving nothing more than a heap of debris, blood stained by those that had been unfortunate enough to be stood on that side of the structure when the accident struck. The cave-in had been instant and devastating, a sight dragged straight from the visions of hell as the speeding petrol tanker had smashed effortlessly through the entrance and exploded on impact with the grand staircase. The driver, busy defending himself from an attack within his cab had been too busy to notice the colossal structure rushing towards him but by the time he glanced up it was too late in more ways than one.

Trying simply to escape he had been blinded by panic, accelerating simply in an effort to get away from the city and at the same time battling with the creature that fought to bite and devour him. He had felt the glass from his windscreen cut into his face at the very same time he had felt the teeth of the infected sink deep into his arm but this had been it for him. Moments after this pain he had been obliterated by the almighty explosion caused by the fuel in his cargo. The detonation tore through the entranceway of the building and all those hundreds that had taken refuge inside, the intense heat from such a confined blaze liquefying those that were caught in its immediate wrath. Hiding away from the army of dead had proven for this handful pointless as the raging flames consumed them and took their lives albeit in a much more humane way than dying at the hands of the surrounding monsters. Immediately after the initial explosion, over a quarter of the whole structure had toppled leaving those that had somehow miraculously survived the blast waiting to be crushed by a million tons of falling concrete and brickwork. It had been a catastrophe of epic proportion, the force alone shattering the windows of buildings that stood over five hundred yards away.

Debris had flown high and far enough to land almost a mile away some of the falling rubble taking out individual zombies although having absolutely no affect on the mass number that the army had reached. The surrounding streets were filled with clouds of dust fog for days after and there were no emergency services to rescue those remaining trapped survivors that had somehow survived the initial blast and the buildings collapse, they were simply stuck until starvation, suffocation or the severe burn wounds took them to a better place. As it was now though the trapped and reachable bodies had been eaten, the fog had settled leaving the crumbled building looking nothing like the monument it had once been although it seemed that the destruction had brought with it something of a positive nature for just a small handful of people. Daniel Shaw, Robert Angel, Shaznay Downes and Paula Dayne were all employed at the theatre and had been working the day of the accident and citywide zombie attacks. Luckily they had all drawn the ushering duties on that God-awful day, every other job unfortunately for everyone else at the theatre had meant working in the lobby, or at least nearby which was where the whole incident had of course taken place.

Being a good group of work friends they had been taking a sneaky fag break in one of the rear facing janitor's rooms when everything had occurred, and it was thanks to their position in the building that they had been the sole survivors of what had proven to be a very costly catastrophe. All four of them had been thrown to the ground through the sheer force of the explosion but apart from a few cuts and scrapes they had all come through with no real damage, unlike the rest of the buildings occupants which they had all found out on inspection to be dead, injured or unreachable. Once they had dusted themselves off and gone out to investigate what had happened, they were greeted with a sight that they would never have imagined possible, it was like they had opened a doorway into another world. It had simply been like looking out onto pure evil.

The burning fire tinted wind blew blisteringly into their faces as they looked out onto Upper Parliament Street, the wall and grand entrance to the building were simply gone along with a large portion of the theatre its self. Robert Angel had managed to mutter the words, "What the fuck!" Before continuing a feeble attempt of trying to absorb what had just occurred and what he was now seeing. Bodies lay everywhere, most of which were burning furiously while the odd scream of the injured and dying could be heard through the roaring petrol fuelled blaze. It had been gut wrenching to look at but like a car crash they had all found it impossible to look away from this giant disaster that they had avoided merely by being in the tiny box room. It was not long before the shocked onlookers saw the first of the zombies scrambling its way onto the rubble, they knew what it was that they were looking at but couldn't accept it as fact because what they were seeing was impossible.

Still it was happening though and it became much more real when the demon that they had seen began to feed on one of the trapped civilians which unfortunately happened to be one of the people that they had worked alongside that very day. It had not mattered how many times they had blinked rapidly or uttered "it can't be" the bizarre and disgusting scenes had continued to unfold in the real life horror film that had begun to take place in front of their very eyes. More creatures soon followed into the disaster zone; eating anyone they came across and in some cases, on the still burning flesh of those involved in the carnage. It was nothing short of hell on earth and despite the horrifying nature of it all, the group couldn't help but continue to stare at the vision before them until the heat of the blaze finally became too much for them to take and they had faced no choice but to retreat back inside.

It had been a long time since that mind-scarring day had happened to the four of them, so long now that they didn't even know what date it was. Their mobile phones had run out of juice weeks before and the only clock that still worked did not have a date function on it. They had given up trying to figure it out, no need for them to know anymore as they had long since realised that no help would be coming to find them.

They had tried the only remaining exit on the first day it had happened but had quickly realised that they had been trapped by these creatures and that had been simply how things had remained. Trapped by these creatures of the dead and by their own fear of what would happen if they even attempted to venture into the outside world.

Paula let out a long sigh as she stuffed a handful of jellybeans into her mouth, wincing at the taste of them and feeling a slight urge to throw up rise in her throat. They had been surviving on fucking cinema snacks for god knows how many weeks now and she couldn't help wonder for how much longer it would sustain them. After all it wasn't exactly the five a day that you supposed to fucking eat, not even close to it for that matter. They were already weak due to the lack of proper nourishment but until now they had not even spoken about attempting to escape; it was a crazy notion while they had the security of the theatre and the food to hand that they did but their haven was no longer looking as good as it had done initially. It was growing a little too much and not just for Paula, she could see it every minute of every day etched into the faces of her companions especially Daniel who had slowly developed a fever over the last few days that had passed.

The group had initially stripped him and checked him for bites despite his resistance but to their relief he had been clean and uninfected. There had of course been no instant where he could have been bitten but there had been no chances taken. They all knew it was probably due to the shit that they had been swallowing every day, facing no real choice but to eat the unhealthy snacks that they had. It was simply pure fucking junk that was in no way what they needed to fuel their bodies sufficiently but apart from facing the zombies, there was very little that they could do about it.

A loud cough echoed round the room, momentarily drowning out the thrum of groans that constantly polluted their ears. Paula, Robert and Shaznay all looked across at the still figure feeling a little more concerned as they did but knowing there was only one possible option should they decide to try and help him. It was obvious that he was dying, of that they were certain but for them to venture out amongst those monsters was surely insane, it would most probably result in all of their deaths, which would not be worthwhile to save the life of just one. This was the logic that they had tried to keep so far knowing that it would make more sense to stay put and to let him die but it was a task a lot easier said than done. He was after all their friend who they did not want to lose and on top of this they were living with the guilt of simply watching him die. It was a situation more fucked up than they had ever imagined possible and it seemed that regardless of what route they decided to take something bad was going to happen and that someone if not all of them were destined to die.

"What the hell are we going to do?" Shaznay said, her voice easing the tension and sadness that had crept over them since they had glanced at their friend who sorrowfully seemed to be growing worse by each passing hour. "If we stay here he fucking dies and if we go out there we probably fucking die, this is bull shit!" She spat the last word, wiping a tear from her cheek but not allowing any more to fall past her glassy green orbs through the fear that they would never stop. The young woman was not even sad any more, sure she had cried once when the fact that her family would be dead had hit home but that was no longer it, it was something else now apart from sadness. She had been stuck in this same place for a couple of months, which had given her more than enough time to grieve but now she was just angry about the whole thing. She felt such hatred towards each of the stumbling, rotting moronic creatures outside and when she looked at Daniel's ashen features it made her blood boil even more so.

It was because of those fucking things that he was dying and it was tearing her apart that she could do very little to resolve this fucked up situation and the fact that she could very easily follow the same path at any given time was just adding fuel to the fire. Because of those bastard things she had been forced to witness and hear so many people die while she had to stand by unable to do anything. She hated it with every fibre of her being and being stuck here watching a friend fade away from lack of real nourishment made it a million times worse. She hoped that at nineteen, the youngest of the group her body would handle the shit diet better than the others but again the thought of being the last survivor did not really bring any form of hope or happiness to her, it would only add solitude to the list of shit that she already had. She just wanted to get out of this mess with or without her friends but she could no longer sit on her arse and do nothing, it was time for her to act she just wished that there was some form of rational infallible plan that she could follow but of course there was no such luxury available to her. Trying to accept the fact that whatever she ended up doing would more than likely kill her was impossible but again the young woman knew that dwelling on her troubled thoughts would only delay her action whatever it was going to be.

    As she stood, Robert and Paula didn't really pay any attention to her movement, Paula was reading the same copy of Heat magazine that she must have read a hundred times and Rob was busy drawing something that resembled a dragon or a big lizard. Shaznay glanced at the two of them and across at the stricken man before she began to speak. "I'm going to make a run for it." Were her only words, which immediately snapped the other two out of their individual activities. "Whether you stay or come it's up to you but I can't take this shit any longer. I am going to pack a few bits of food and some water and leave in about an hour." She looked at the two gawping faces, a little amused, as it was the exact reaction that she had expected before turning and walking towards the room where the rations were kept. She hadn't expected an answer, nor would she chase them for one, she had made up her mind albeit hastily and it was up to them if they wanted to risk everything to try and discover the haven of rescue and of course a decent fucking meal.

    Part of her ashamedly was actually wondering if she would be better chancing things alone though, she was young, fit and strong so it was certainly possible that company would slow her down. Rob was in his early forties and not exactly fit where Paula although only twenty-five seemed like she could become a hindrance due to her fragile emotional state and finally, Daniel pretty much spoke for himself. He was in his thirties and trim enough but in the unconscious state he was in, he was going nowhere. Whichever way it turned out though she would accept it, they were her friends and a helping hand could certainly be needed should she get into any trouble with those fucking things outside but she also accepted the fact that outside it very well would be survival of the fittest.

Rob and Paula had not needed long to debate the course of action that they would take after absorbing the comments that their friend had just made. The thought of leaving the place that had been their home for the past few months had crossed their minds with more and more frequency as the days passed by but up until ten minutes before no one had actually spoken out loud about it. The fear of what lay outside had seen to their silence and to the fact that so far they had stayed put. They were glad that Shaznay had finally broken the quiet on this subject though, the building in which they had held their refuge seemed to be growing smaller and smaller as time crept by almost smothering them. This, combined with the fact that they now faced the death of one of their companions should they choose to take no form of action certainly aided their decision on the matter at hand although they couldn't shed the many doubts that they had about venturing outside. Despite the colossal amount of fear that surrounded the whole notion of an attempted escape seeing how much Daniel was suffering had made up their minds about what they would do, if they chose to stay they knew it would only be a matter of time before they ended up the same. With a mutual nod of their heads and the comment of,

"Come on then, let's go pack," leaving the lips of Robert the two of them rose and followed slowly in the direction of Shaznay.

As they entered the storeroom they received a welcoming smile from her as she accepted the fact that she would be joined on her journey. Despite the previous thoughts of faring better alone she was actually quite glad that they would be with her. It had been a very bold thought to think that she could possibly fight her way through this hell alone and she knew that any help would be good help.

It took the trio ten minutes to pack all that they would need and a further half hour to gather a few weapons which included two broom handles, a truncheon from one of the security guards whose upper body had been crushed by falling debris and a fire extinguisher which they knew they may still need either to pass by some of the flames that were still burning throughout the city or even to be used in self defence. Once they knew it was now or never they paid a last visit to Daniel but they could no longer arouse any form of conscious state within him, his fever had taken over and they all knew that unless they found help fast he would surely die. He was a good friend and she did not want anything to happen to him and she was now more aware than ever that probably ever second would count.

Shaznay poured a small amount of water through his cracked lips and kissed him softly on the forehead before standing and heading back towards the emergency exit at the back of the building, which they knew had been unharmed by the explosion. It was a thick steel door, which had held firm and secure throughout the whole ordeal, but a simple push of the release bar was all it took for it to swing open and bathe the inhabitants with sunlight from outside. The car park thankfully was not too infested with the dead but they knew this would not be the case everywhere; it was only as Paula asked, "Where to now?" That they realised they had not even discussed which direction that they would take in their attempt at finding help or rescue.

Noticing that a few of the closest groaning cadavers had spotted them and were limping their way closer Robert quickly took the initiative and told the girls to follow him and headed of briskly towards the far right hand side of the car park. The women knew immediately that this would lead them towards the police station so no complaints were made about this decision that had been impulsively taken. They just hoped that they either found someone alive or at least some way that they could be rescued and send some help to their dying friend. Either way they were momentarily happy knowing that the building that they sought was less than half a mile away and would more than likely contain radios and a better selection of weapons than what they currently had. It was a faint hope, but a hope non-the less.

"Thy dead men shall live, together with my dead body shall they arise. Awake and sing, ye that dwell in dust: for thy dew is as the dew of herbs, and the earth shall cast out the dead."
Isaiah 26:19

Chapter 5

The noise woke him with a jolt. Panting heavily he wasn't sure if he had imagined the sound or if it had indeed been real. His mind swam through the haziness of sleep as he tried to wake up faster than his body could physically allow him to. As his vision became clearer he glanced at the glass of whiskey that had tumbled from his grip and spun his head quickly to ensure his kitchen barricade was still in place, which he found to his relief that it was. As his sleepy eyes and hung over mind swam slowly in and out of focus and he stood upright on his aching legs the sound rang out once again confirming that it was indeed authentic and not a part of his unconscious imagination. Despite his bewildered half conscious state a smile immediately spread across his bristled face as he accepted this intrusion as the sweetest sound he had heard in a long time. It was the distinct sound of gunfire, which he knew could only mean that there were other survivors and they were fucking close too. Not only that, they were properly armed which compared to his shovel was certainly a big deal. He knew immediately that he would now have to leave the confines of his home and venture outside to try and track down the source of the sound but he no longer had a fear of this venture or what would be lurking in the outdoors. The devastation that he felt from losing his partner overwhelmed any sense of dread that he held for the zombies, which he hoped, would help him on his mission to find these survivors that by the sound of things were not too far from his house. He just hoped that he could see through the burning anger that he still felt so that he could at least fight with some form of clarity in his mind.

With a rush of energy that he didn't know that he had, Frank Garred flew up the flight of stairs and into his bedroom grabbing the hold-all that he had packed over a month ago just in case a situation like this should arise. Once again being prepared would pay off it seemed as he ran over to the big bay window that overlooked the main road to the front of his house. He knew that the in the time it could take him to pack some rations and supplies the opportunity to join other survivors could quite easily pass him by which he was certainly not willing to risk. As he peered out into the gloomy early morning light his sight was automatically drawn to the number of ghouls skulking around below, it would be difficult to get past them but with the speed and agility that he knew very well he possessed, he was confident he could avoid their attempts to feed on him. If he didn't there was of course only one outcome but he was willing to take his fucking chances rather than remain cooped up and alone for the rest of his existence, besides that he knew that his food supply would eventually run out so leaving was a simple inevitability.

As he began to quickly estimate the number of zombies he would have to pass another deafening gunshot bellowed out and this time he knew exactly how close these survivors were. From the very corner of his peripheral vision he had seen the distant muzzle flash, like an orange flame illuminating not only the dark but also the hopes of survival within Frank himself. Without even giving it more than a seconds thought he belted back the way he came taking the stairs three at a time before retrieving his trusty spade from the kitchen hoping that it would continue to serve him as well as it had so far. He knew without double-checking that these people whoever they may be would have gone into the schoolyard for the safety that it would more than likely offer. Thinking about it now he couldn't help but wonder why he hadn't tried to make it there himself before now, after all it did have a giant fence surrounding it, which he assumed, was what had drawn the newcomer or newcomers towards the building. Either way though it mattered little what reason they had for being near his house, it was time to make a move and try to join them.

The three of them stood unmoving in the gloom as they waited to see if another noise would come, seconds ticked agonizingly by but all that followed was that constant groaning that tainted the air everywhere they went.

"Come on, let's go." Were Matt's simple words as he stepped into the huge building knowing that this person that he assumed was a woman may probably need saving in a hurry. The other two followed, all of them now moving stealthily and keeping on guard preparing for anything that may be thrown at them. Guns at the ready though they were confident that they could deal with whatever lay ahead, they had survived this fucking far so they just carried on with things assuming that they would continue to do so. They hoped of course that the building was deserted as far as the creatures went but going by the scream that had just erupted they fucking doubted it. Matt kept the lead while Sean took the rear, checking each room as they moved slowly down the long corridor that had met them upon their entry. The first four doors to be checked were identical classrooms, set out in exactly the same way apart from the posters that hung in each of them as they seemed relevant to whatever was taught inside. Thankfully each of these rooms were uninhabited which was a trend that they hoped would continue along their search.

Abbey was glad someone else had taken the lead inside the school, she was happy that they were away from all the monsters outside but she still couldn't help the feeling of danger shrouding her despite the new surroundings. She knew that should anything happen she had two men by her side that would fight to the death to save her as she would for them but she couldn't help the uncontrollable sense that something was very seriously wrong. As she saw Matt slowly open the fifth door that they approached she tried to mentally shake the mood that seemed to grip her telling herself that they would be perfectly safe and that they would hopefully find this survivor in time to help them and of course happily add the new uninfected addition to their little group. She tried to force a slight smile to herself in an effort to shake away the dread but within the space of one of her rapid heartbeats, the fear that she had felt was suddenly and brutally confirmed.

Matthew's entrance into the room came to an abrupt stop as his body went rigid in front of his companion's eyes. Wondering what had halted his forward movement, time seemed to stand still as they waited for him to say something or at least waited for a noise to come from the room but for three seconds, which to them seemed like an eternity nothing happened. Sean began to raise his hand, wanting to find out what the hell had just come over his friend but he received his answer before he had the chance to even touch him. Matthew Hughes's statuesque body fell backwards like a tree falling in the woods as his skull smashed into the floor with a nauseating thud the sickening truth slapped them in the face. Another scream erupted bouncing off the corridor walls but this time the noise came from Abbey as she looked at the glistening silver handle protruding from the fallen man's face. Sean jumped back as if he had been hit by lightening unable to comprehend what had just happened but at the same time knowing that he had to react immediately, he couldn't risk the same fate for himself and Abbey by standing around in a panic.

The door had now swung shut once again but still no moans came from within which along with the knife that had instantly killed his good friend made the situation bewildering to the two stunned onlookers. Sean quickly took a step to the side avoiding the pool of blood that had formed around the body of Matthew before thumping his size twelve boot into the wooden surface with as much force as he could humanly muster. It swung open with a might he didn't even know he possessed and it certainly had the desired effect. He saw in a flash that the room was a small narrow kitchen and it appeared at first that it was empty but as the door thundered round on its hinges the lack of a loud crack as the handle should have hit the back wall gave it all away. He heard the sound of a pain filled feminine groan as the door hit home before it swung back closed once again, the sound that followed a few moments after once again told him exactly what he needed to know and giving him the indication that it was time to move. Whoever it was that had stabbed Matthew was hopefully now immobile which gave him the few seconds he needed to safely get inside and take control of this suddenly deadly situation.

What he had expected considering the knife and the dead form of his friend he had not even had time to contemplate but the sight of a fourteen year old girl unconscious on the ground would probably not have been his first rational guess. He couldn't believe it, this tiny female creature had just murdered his friend and there was nothing he could do about it now. He was shell-shocked, for the first time since this shit had all begun he was rooted to the spot and completely stumped, lost for both words and actions. They had survived so fucking much and now this shit had happened and taken one of them so cruelly. What the fuck were they supposed to do now? He hoped Abbey had an answer because he sure as shit didn't, he just didn't know how to react to this stunning incident. Hearing how much she was sobbing behind him though he doubted that she would have a solution, he doubted it very much.

The giant woman had still been where he had last left her, trying with every ounce of will she had to wedge her enormous form through the small gap between the gate and the side of Frank's house. The sight had once again amused him which considering what was happening everywhere was a little sadistic that he could still muster up enjoyment at a fat person getting stuck in a small gap. "Some things will always be funny," were the words he had spoken to himself before shearing through her neck with the edge of his spade enabling a free passageway to the street.

The blood that had spattered his t-shirt mattered little to him despite the fact that it was his favourite one. The Guns n Roses memorabilia held no value for Frank at the moment, his one and only will to reach the other survivor or survivors that were so close he could almost taste them. Besides should he ever get through this he was quite sure he could get a new one but he had many more pressing issues at the moment than a fashion calamity as he took a cautious step out onto the street. He looked to his right, happy that the nearest demon was a good twenty feet away and then turned to his left towards the school. There were at least thirty of the fuckers between him and where he was headed but he knew that he could make it and that if not he would certainly take some of the bastards down in his attempt to reach the building. At the top of his voice he let out an almighty scream and ran towards the first zombie with his spade held high. It was the first time that he realised that he was no longer doing this solely as an attempt to survive; he wanted to kill as many of them as he could. He would avenge Sharon and that was a promise he made to himself there and then, the more of the bastards he killed before they got to him the better.

Chapter 6

Paula screamed as another one attempted to grab her, some of the rotting skin breaking loose on her shirt as she managed to avoid the lunging beast by mere inches. They had only managed a few hundred yards before they had been greeted by thousands of the swarming dead, the safety of the theatre suddenly seeming like a sanctuary unlike only moments before. Everywhere that they looked there seemed to be more of them and certainly no easy route to take in order for them to reach their intended target, the urge to simply panic taking over rapidly. Although the police station was so close it appeared now that they could have bitten off more than they could chew and it was for this purpose that Paula now began tugging frantically on the back of Robert's jumper, her fear beginning to control every aspect of her thoughts.

Shaznay now led the way, swinging the truncheon wildly at an oncoming figure smiling to herself through the fear as she heard its skull crumble under the impact of her blow. Despite the frightening fear of death that she felt surprisingly a part of her felt exhilarated that she was actually doing something now, trying to battle the problem and save a friend in need as opposed to the constant waiting that they had endured for so long. With lightening footwork she almost danced between cadavers and attacked only those that she couldn't evade, her one thought to try and save herself and the three solitary people that she had left in the whole world. As she floored another monster this time with a swift kick to the shins a shriek erupted from behind her making her automatically swivel and look as she hoped that her friends were safe and that they hadn't fallen behind. Time seemed to stand still as she spun, dreadfully expecting to see them swamped by monsters but the sight that greeted her was far worse, it made her feel sick in the instant that she struggled to accept what she saw. They were fucking leaving her. The two people who she had called friends and whom she was fighting to save were running back to the theatre and not for one second had they called for her to join them. They had simply left her to die amongst the mass of zombies without a second thought.

Her emotions raged as she saw the two figures disappearing, fury, sadness and a complete emptiness came over her as Shaznay struggled to accept what the hell she was seeing. There was simply no mistaking it, they had left her completely alone and it destroyed her as she felt the emptiness tearing her apart within. "Mother fuckers!" Echoed after the two fleeing shapes as she screamed the two words with all her might but as a massive weight suddenly hit her from behind and as the concrete rushed up to meet her face she knew she had let her guard down for a moment too long.

The anger and hate were instantly replaced with a dizziness that threatened to take away her conscious state as her head slammed into the tarmac with a thud that she was unable to stop. The whole incident happening so fast she simply hadn't possessed the speed in order to cushion the savage fall. She grunted from the impact and felt warmth on her face as blood began to flow freely from two wounds that had opened from the blow. It was thankfully her instinct to survive that took over though as she thrashed her arms and began to kick free the fiend that held her back and threatened to end her life. Through her haze she prayed that the fucker wouldn't get chance to bite her and it was as she felt the weight shift and she scrambled to her feet that it seemed her prayer had been answered although the weakness she felt was more than a worry.

On unsteady legs she turned and threw a wild hook at this thing that had grabbed her, instantly sickened and repulsed by its severely decayed appearance. Half of this man's face had been torn free along with all of his bottom jaw, which was probably the reason she had managed to avoid a fatal bite. A thick yellow fluid bubbled from within the eye sockets and its stench was massively intrusive making her feel quite ill from both the appearance and the rank odour that she had to withstand. Luckily the first shot had the desired effect as her small but solid fist pulverised the monsters neck, the rotting flesh that remained on her skin afterwards made her retch but Shaznay managed to keep her wits and instantly began running as fast as she could ignoring the throbbing pain from her injuries. No point in waiting to see if she had killed the fucking thing, she knew there was any time to stand still while she was stranded outside on her own, she had just made that mistake and it had almost cost her everything. There were so many monsters and because of this she had made a very quick decision, which through sheer spirit and fight took her in the opposite direction to the two cowards who had just left her alone to die. Fuck them both she thought as her legs powered forward her instinct once more helping her dodge what seemed like hundreds of attempted attacks from the surrounding bodies that all wanted to feast on her.

Thankfully the truncheon that she held continued to come in very useful on those that came a little too close for comfort, their rotting bodies no match for the solid metal implement which she seemed to use with such an accuracy as though it was an extension of her arm. As she rounded a bend and floored another one of the flesh hungry fiends she slowed to a stop as a smile spread widely across her bloodstained face. Only two hundred yards ahead stood the building she had been looking for and to her delight it seemed still perfectly intact, it wasn't burned or destroyed, it looked exactly as it should have done. It looked perfect. Nottinghamshire Police Station were the words plastered across the sign and it was a glorious sight for Shaznay, she badly needed refuge and a chance to rest as she began running once more despite her already laboured breathing and the continuous pain in her skull from her brush with the tarmac.

It took her another couple of minutes to navigate her way through the swarms of undead managing thankfully to remain unbitten and another thirty seconds after this to pick the lock on one of the supposed security doors round the back of the building. It seemed her few years of petty teenage crime had paid off as she replaced her hair grip and entered cautiously noticing immediately the eerie silence as she was faced by a long seemingly empty corridor. As she looked both ways, closing the door securely behind her it didn't take long for her to notice the smell and the fact that one of the walls was heavily spattered with crimson. Suddenly the building didn't seem as secure as she had first thought and her hopes were not as high as they had initially been. Shaznay could only assume that she certainly wasn't alone inside the station and it was with this daunting thought that she prepared to search.

Tears streamed down her cheeks, soaking Roberts shoulder as Paula continued to sob unable to control the emotions that flooded from within. He sustained his attempts trying to tell her that they would have died if they had continued and that they had done the right thing but he knew his words were completely useless and not only that they were lies. They were both complete and utter heartless bastards that had left a good friend not only to die but also to die in the worse possible way. She would be eaten alive and the worse thing was when Paula had told him she wanted to go back he hadn't even hesitated on grabbing her hand and turning his back on Shaznay. They had no excuse for what they had done and no words that were spoken could make them feel any differently about what had happened and what the consequences would be. They may as well have killed her themselves.

On arrival back at the theatre, Robert had dragged the hysterical Paula with him back to the place they knew so well. Their other friend Daniel as expected still lay as they had left him and unsurprisingly he still looked like shit warmed up. His skin was ghostly white and his lips were tinged a horrible shade of blue, which made the fact that the two of them had given up even more unbearable, thanks to them he would now most certainly die and by the looks of things in the not too distant future.. Not only did they have to accept the circumstances that they had left with Shaznay but they now had to face another person's impending death too. The guilt that they felt was so immense but even with that they both knew that they were not about to go running back out there in a magical attempt to save the day, they just didn't have it in them and on top of this it was probably already too late.

As Robert stroked her hair in an effort to try and stop her crying he looked across once more at Daniel and tried to accept that they would now have to watch over him until his very last breath. They would remain here in the theatre in the slim hope that help would come before they themselves died but the thought of that occurring before he did was pretty much impossible. Looking at his ashen features, Robert honestly wondered if he would make it through the day before he finally gave up and let death take him. It was bad and he knew that it would soon be much worse as they would have to move the body once he had passed away. As the disturbing thoughts of carrying out such a task spun through his head an almighty rumble tore through the building shaking everything around the two of them so strongly he feared that the rest of the building may have been giving way and collapsing around them. Startled, Paula's wailing turned instantly to a whimper as she clung tightly to Robert and looked around the room not knowing what to expect. Seconds ticked by although not much seemed to have happened in the room where they sat apart from the odd badly balanced item that had fallen but they both knew that something serious had just occurred nearby.

   It took a few moments to gather their nerves but both rose together and hand in hand once more they approached the door and slowly opened it before heading once again to the exit through which they had only just returned. With everything that had unfolded around them over the last months they always expected the impossible to happen but the sight that greeted them outside took them both by surprise. Despite the fact that they were on ground level the only thing outside for fifty feet was a gaping hundred foot deep hole. The car park on which they had earlier walked had simply disappeared.

   It was so fucking quiet, even barefoot each step made a noise down the hallway in which she still stood. A giant explosion of some kind had rung through the air only moments before shaking the structure around her but she didn't want to venture back out to see what the hell it was. She had seen quite enough of the outside world for one day that was for sure and so long as the explosion didn't affect her she didn't really care. The deafening blast had made her jump for sure but thankfully no creatures within her vicinity had been alerted and the room had remained so far inhabited only by her. She had chosen to go left convincing herself that it was the best route as it seemed the longest although she knew it had been chosen simply due to the fact it seemed more appealing than the blood spattered direction. Caution and fear had taken over the hatred that she had felt for her friends for now as she peeked into the first room that she came across. It was the staff room and thankfully apart from snack machines and the usual paraphernalia that would be expected it was completely deserted. Shaznay walked across to the fridge and inspected the contents cringing a little as the door groaned loudly on its hinges. After listening to make sure no one or nothing had heard, she was more than happy to find an unopened bottle of Coke which she helped herself to, thirstily drinking half of the contents in one go enjoying the refreshing cold liquid as it made its way to her stomach.

Although the distance between the theatre and her current location wasn't that far the amount of zombie dodging she had done probably meant she had run at least twice the distance and expended a hell of a lot more energy. She was tired and in pain but she knew that she had to inspect the station regardless of how she felt as she dabbed at the congealing blood on her face. Gasping a little from the amount of liquid she had just swallowed, Shaznay took a minute to study the room a little more clearly. She was glad to notice that the drink and food machines both seemed heavily stocked so nourishment would not be an issue for the near future at least. She didn't know if she could use her hair grip to pick the strange circular locks that held them shut but worse came to the worse she would just put her foot through the glass front if she needed the contents within.

She studied the walls noting various pieces of information about staff training and parties that meant nothing to her but thankfully near the doorway was exactly what she needed. The map of the station was priceless especially knowing what could be lurking in any of the rooms in this building, the blood stained corridor outside had already confirmed that she certainly had to keep her guard up and be alert for attacks that she knew could come from pretty much anywhere. The last thing she needed was to have to search each room individually too so she was thanking the heavens that she had discovered this, which would keep her on the right path to the things that she sought. She sat for a moment taking another drink as she studied the paper that she now held. It turned out that she had been heading the right way and that after passing the next two doors on her left, which were closets and classrooms she would reach the first of two places that she was looking for. The weapons storage although most likely locked was well worth checking and as it was the closest of the necessary rooms to her. After the first point of call she wanted the communications room although she had noticed that this room was upstairs and would take quite a walk as it lay on the opposite side of the building to where she was.

   The other visit she planned on making was the canteen, although not a necessity it was on the way to the communications room and she wanted something proper to eat. Anything would taste like heaven to her after eating sweets and popcorn for two months so she was praying for at least some form of a real meal as opposed to the crap that had constituted as her diet since all this shit began. Unfortunately the machine in the room where she stood held nothing of real interest to her as it was the same garbage that she had been eating since the beginning so the trip to the canteen was something that she was now looking forward to.

   Apart from that there was little on the map that she paid attention to for now, there was no need really. So long as she became properly armed and tried to get rescue that was all that mattered to her at the moment, she would worry about any other rooms should her first plan not work but she hoped with all her might that it would not come to that.

   Shaznay drank what was left in her bottle before rolling the map and placing it in the side pocket of her combats, she was certainly ready to be rescued and to get away from this fucked up mess that was for sure and now without those gutless bastards with her she only had that solitary task to focus on. With a deep breath and a mind full of determination she began to head towards the corridor, she was prepared for anything.

Chapter 7

They had waited a while for the young girl to regain consciousness, Abbey eventually managing to control her tears at the sudden loss of Matthew knowing that she needed as ever to remain strong despite the devastating loss that they had just unexpectedly had to face. Admittedly she had lost people much closer to her before now so she had at least managed to force herself to shake this newest tragedy from the front of her mind so that she could focus on the current situation along with Sean. They had both known without having to speak to the stranger that she had acted only out of fear and self-defence that was for sure, it was just another fucked up situation that had thrown its self at them and sadly it had resulted in the death that they now struggled to cope with. The unfortunate aspect being that there was no resolution to this problem, no one at whom they could aim their anger and sadness apart from the hordes of corpses outside.

They sat facing the young girl; Abbey simply held her hand in an effort to try and reassure her and gain some trust after what had just happened. The girl was shocked from being knocked unconscious and with what had happened to Matthew but that was expected, she had after all just killed someone and not only that she had been alone in this place. What she must have had to face combined with the act she had just committed would be a hard thing for anyone to accept never mind someone as young as her.

After a few minutes of slow conversation with the girl, it soon became apparent that she had been separated from her parents at the school gates during an escape attempt; they had pushed her inside as the creatures had devoured them and this horror that she had been through showed on her face and in her actions. The poor thing looked exhausted and trembled constantly although after seeing what she had at her age neither Sean nor Abbey could blame her for seeming so fragile. She was thankfully more than happy to speak to them it was just taking time, the strains of what she had endured weighing heavily on such a young mentality as she struggled to cope with it all and express the many things that she had trapped in her mind. On top of this they had no idea how long she had been cooped up in the school alone to cope with the memories of watching her parent's unfortunate demise, they could only begin to imagine what it must have been like for her. The solitude, the memories and the constant thrum of the dead, Sean and Abbey couldn't believe she still had her sanity never mind her life.

"What's your name sweetie?" Were the words softly spoken by Sean, Abbey for the first time hearing a calm, sweet side to the large man, which despite the situation took her by surprise.

"Rhianne." Was the single softly spoken one word response that they received but it was enough, it was all that they wanted from her. One sentence at a time, slowly but surely they would gain her trust so that she knew they were there to help her through the mess that surrounded them. They were just happy that she was talking to them and that they had found another survivor although this discovery had come at a devastating loss.

"My ribs hurt." Were the next noises that came from the girl, every word a mere whisper and thanks to the thump she had taken from the door it seemed she could easily have a couple of cracks or breaks. She leaned forward and let the two of them take a look wincing as she did so at the fresh wave of pain that the movement brought with it. Thankfully, on a simple inspection the initial bruising was not too severe however it still looked pretty painful and would possibly slow down her movement especially if they had to get anywhere at speed. Sean immediately felt wracked with guilt at the sight, apologising for being the cause of her discomfort, although knowing that he had faced no choice in his actions at the time.

"That's ok," she responded covering her side back up again. "I am sorry I killed your friend, I thought he was a monster though and he would kill me. I was really frightened." She continued, tears brimming in her massive blue eyes as she thought of what had happened once more, the fact that she had killed someone beginning to sink in to her fragile mind especially when she glanced down and saw the specs of blood that covered one of her hands. Sean leant forward and rested his giant hand on her arm, the warmth of the contact seeming to calm her somewhat and stop the pending flood of tears that were only moments away. He quickly explained that her actions were only what anyone would have done and that she need not worry, they certainly didn't blame her for what she had done. "We will keep you safe and try and get help." He finished before standing and heading towards the door. "I will go find you some pain killers for those ribs while you stay here and keep Abbey Company, ok?" He asked smiling as she frantically nodded her head at him before he cautiously went back into the hall where his dead friend still lay, the pool of blood beginning to congeal in the heated hallway in a sight that still looked so surreal he struggled to accept it.

He immediately pushed back thoughts of Matt's death, thinking instead that Rhianne already seemed to be loosening up, and for that simple bliss he was so relieved. He knew that as always looking at the positives rather than the negatives of the situation would help things. He couldn't help but feel for her too after what the poor thing had been through trapped here alone but one thing was for sure, he would do all he could to ensure that she remained safe and that she didn't have to see anyone else be torn apart by these things. On that note he would ensure that Abbey remained in his protection too, he had lost enough people now and that was the end of it as far as he was concerned, the unfortunate accident had simply been something that he had not been able to control. To protect them both he would carry out a sweep of the building while looking for some painkillers and so long as all was clear there was no reason that they couldn't survive here safely for quite some time.

Abbey watched her friend leave the room, his large frame disappearing out of sight before she turned and took a seat on the floor next to their newest compatriot. Despite her own fragile nature she knew that this girl needed comfort after all that she had been through and what was still occurring all around couldn't be helping things. It was simply amazing that she had survived so far and even more remarkable that she had managed to remain sane throughout the horror and evil that she must have dealt with. As Starks placed her arm around the young teenager, she sank happily into her loving warm embrace, the force with which she held her arm letting Abbey know just how scared and glad for contact she was. A single tear rolled down the adult's cheek, unsure if it was for the loss of her own family or if it was shed compassionately for the losses that Rhianne had endured it trickled down leaving a trail behind on her soft skin.

She gripped the girl tighter and reassured her that all would be ok despite her own insecurities about survival, at least for now though she felt the safest she had in a long while and in this embrace probably the happiest too. She lifted her left hand to wipe away the dampness beneath her eyes and as she did so two noises erupted in the corridor outside making both of the girls jump simultaneously. The first had been an eerie groan coming from what they knew had to have been a zombie and the second was a deafening sound of gunfire. It was as the silence returned Abbey remembered that on entry to the school, the girl had let out a scream and that they had obviously forgotten about this all through the mayhem and confusion. She knew that Sean had found the cause of the scream; she just hoped and prayed that he had dealt with it in a manner that had left him uninjured and uninfected. She had faith in his abilities though and with that thought she simply applied more pressure in her embrace with Rhianne and whispered once more that everything would be ok.

He was panting heavily and his clothes were drenched with sweat and the blood of at least fifteen zombies. His back was pressed up against a large oak tree as he looked on at the wildly flailing arms trying to reach through the gate and grab at his warm perspiration soaked flesh. He spat angrily at the three cadavers, the urge to return and attack them burning like a wildfire within but he knew he had been more than fortunate to make it as far as he had besides which he was completely exhausted. Frank Garred had reached the school, the safety that he needed and also the place where he knew the other survivor or survivors were. He had not for one moment considered how much energy it would take to accomplish what he had but either way he made it and despite his shaky legs he knew that he had to continue. As he turned to examine his surroundings he was a little surprised at how small it appeared, trees from the street hid the majority of the building and having no children he had never had the need to really investigate or come near this place. All he knew was there was at least one person inside and that this person had a fucking heartbeat and a gun and it was this that was his simple sole focus. He supposed though that the fact that the school was so bloody little at least meant it would be a damn sight easier to find whoever it was inside.

Garred stood up straight and peered momentarily into the gloom of the playground to his right, he couldn't hear any groans from that direction and so far it certainly appeared that he had entered a zombie free zone for which he was ecstatic. He knew caution would have to be taken though after all the noise from the corpses behind him could quite easily drown out the sounds of zombies ahead. It was as he took his first step towards the doorway ahead that he heard the crack of gunfire and the room to the right of the front door lit up revealing a sight that he certainly had not wanted to see. The vision of a large man attempting to fend off an attacking demon burned itself into his retinas as he burst into a sprint, dropping his bag knowing the only thing he would need to help was his spade and his animal instincts. He just hoped that he would round the corner in time to help or that the poor bastard would get off a better shot than the first one had seemed to be. Frank thrust his shoulder through the main door like a madman ignoring the pain that came with his action, he did the same with the second seeing pretty much exactly what he had expected. The creature was on top of this survivor its rotting gums and teeth snapping wildly as it tried to bite into his flesh beneath.

"Hold his head up!" Were the only words that he shouted, spade aloft ready to swing and thankfully the man complied within a split second, hoisting the zombie as high as he possibly could. The weapon sliced through the creature's neck easily, the frantic struggle ending in an instant leaving Sean to push the thankfully lifeless corpse away so that he could stand once more. It took some effort but he regained his footing shaking his head as he did so. "Fucker came out of nowhere, I just couldn't shake the bastard." He said, taking Franks hand and shaking it vigorously to thank this new comer for saving his life. At the same time he couldn't help gawp his surprise at the fact yet another survivor had appeared and not only that had he not suddenly entered the room, his battle with the zombie could have cost him his life.

They exchanged introductions, Garred immediately asking Sean if he was the only survivor, thrilled when he discovered there were two more waiting in another room and giving his instant condolences when he heard about the very recent death of Matthew. Rather than exchange in depth stories and waste time, they agreed it was best to go back and let the two girls know all was ok but they would sweep the remaining rooms on the way to be as safe as they could be. There were five more in all, a giant cafeteria that seemed to be stocked with enough food to see an army through a month and some more classes with a staff room to finish off the two men's search. All were thankfully empty as far as the living dead were concerned and as they entered the kitchen where the girls had been left Sean was delighted to see them in the same spot although this time Abbey was pointing a gun in his direction and both of them looked quite flustered which he had kind of expected after the gunfire that had come from his battle with the zombie.

"What the hell happened, are you ok?" Were the frantic words that spilled from her lips as she lowered the gun, Sean smiling at her and happy to see that she was so worried about him. He walked over and hugged her, giving a second cuddle to Rhianne before explaining his near death encounter and the entrance of Frank the sudden hero who remained stood in the doorway with a smile on his face and his blood spattered spade in his hand. Sean continued to explain that the other rooms had been checked and that all was now clear along with the fact that they had a shit load of food to keep them nice and happy which lit up Abbey's face immediately, she was starving and as she expected Sean must be too. Without even discussing it the group made their way over to the canteen, Frank locking the main doors as they passed them just as a precaution should the gates outside not be as secure as they first appeared. After all one zombie had made its way inside and even

Rhianne couldn't shed any light on how stable the surrounding fence was having spent all of her time within the school hiding.

Before doing anything else, deservedly the four of them sat and ate, quite happily exchanging conversation and enjoying the nice easy atmosphere before the two men ventured out and examined the school grounds in more detail, happily finding that they were now certainly the only ones inside. They moved Matt's body outdoors agreeing that he would be buried the following morning, Franks spade and some other garden tools they had found would be sufficient for this task that they certainly weren't looking forward to. It seemed too on further inspection that the fences around were also indeed just as secure as they had thought. Trees mainly blocked any access to the surrounding fence and those parts that weren't shaded by woodland were steady and strong. It seemed that the zombies would not be getting inside at any point soon and that finally they could all feel safe and secure for at least a while. For once it seemed something good had actually happened for them all and they hoped that their fortune would continue.

Chapter 8

It was fucking unlocked! Although she knew the chances of anything remaining within were pretty low as she nudged the door slowly open, the anticipation that she felt simply unbearable. The fucking place had more than likely been ransacked as soon as all this shit had started but still it was worth a look as she peered into the gloom listening for any signs of danger from both within and at the same time from behind her. The last thing she wanted was to go running in all excited and giddy just to get mauled by one of those dead fucking things, she had come to far now to let a careless moment cost her everything.

On top of that she knew that she had to keep her wits about her, one of those things could quite easily creep up on her whilst she was distracted which was another situation that she didn't want to find herself in. She would do everything safely and as enough time passed for her to feel secure she pressed blindly three times on the wall to her right before locating the switch that bathed the room in light. She squinted at first as her vision sparkled somewhat but her first instinct was surprise and absolute joy as she stared at the many items that were facing her within the room. There were guns, ammo vests and a shit load of truncheons staring straight at her, it was unbelievable, she had hit the bloody jackpot. It seemed that amidst the panic, chaos and death of the entire police force these items had been left behind, perhaps in case of a retreat that never happened but whatever the reason for her fortune she could only be thankful.

She smiled hugely as she approached the shotgun at the opposite end of the room, it glistened in the light and as she shouldered the heavy weapon it made her feel so much safer than the tiny little baton that she had survived with so far although she had grown quite fond of the small hand held weapon. After all it was thanks to this that she had made it from the theatre safely and without being eaten. As she ecstatically examined further, there were plenty of shells next to the shotgun, which made her next action quite a simple one. She poured out the contents of one box thumbing two cartridges into the weapon first before cocking it shut and chambering one of them ready to fire at anything that fucking moved or even made a noise. Despite her previous fear of the undead creatures a part of her actually wanted one of the stinking bastards to stumble in now.

Unloading a cartridge into the face of one of those fuckers seemed already like it would be a very satisfying task. After admiring the weapon for quite some time, she placed the gun down before removing her tattered white t-shirt, enjoying the air conditioning on her almost naked upper body for a moment before retrieving one of the bulletproof vests near to where she stood. Shaznay sighed a little as she looked down at herself, her skin was dirty and the bra that she wore had bloodstains on the left strap and breast cup. She knew that she was lucky to be alive and all that but still she couldn't help but wish she were soaking in a hot bath and realising that this were all one giant fucked up dream. Sadly though that was not to be so she shook away the momentary feeling of sadness and placed her arms into the vest before filling the pockets with as much ammo as she could carry. She was not about to run out at any point and despite feeling over stocked she was not about to risk anything by taking too little, better safe than fucking sorry that was for sure when everywhere you looked there were flesh hungry zombies. Next she took one of the automatic pistols, clumsily removing the magazine so that she could locate some more of the same ammunition.

Despite the odd naughty deed as a teen she was certainly not familiar with weapons so this was a learning curve that she knew she would have to pick up fast. The shotgun had been simple enough, she had seen them used so many times in the movies however the hand gun did prove a little trickier as she eventually tracked down the replacement ammo and slid three mags into one of the police belts which she also placed on her body. In the silence of the room she actually allowed herself a small giggle as she caught sight of her appearance in a dusty mirror towards the back of the room. "Lock and load." She said smiling unable to stop thinking that seeing herself armed up to the teeth was so surreal and that fact that it looked a little like fancy dress gone extreme didn't help either. She knew though that being dressed this way was in no way a laughing matter and that it was as serious as it could possibly be, she accepted after all that the ammo she carried would in fact have to be used at some point probably not too far away. As her amusement subsided she glanced around one more time, pocketing a small blade although with her guns she doubted she would need it before pulling the map from her pocket once again. There was nothing more worth taking from here for now so her next trip would be to the canteen on route to the radio room, she just needed to make sure she didn't make any wrong turns on her way as she glanced at the sheet purely for a jog of her memory.

The building was a big fucker and the last thing she needed was to get herself lost when she was pretty damn sure that there was something nasty lurking somewhere after seeing the bloodstained wall on her entry to the station. On top of this though she didn't want to waste the vital energy that getting lost would take, she was shattered as it was so the quicker she reached her targets the better it would be and the sooner she would be able to rest. As she made a mental note that she would pass three more rooms before the stairway to the next floor, which was where she wanted to be she heard the first noise since she had been inside the station. At first she wondered if it could have been the wind but she knew better than that, it was one of them things but thankfully for the first time she was more than ready for the bastards. Shaznay pocketed the map once again and left the room with a confidence in her step that she knew came from her newfound weapons rather than her ability to deal with the monsters.

As she turned to her left she immediately saw the source of the groan she had heard and as expected it was one of the living dead stumbling slowly in her direction. With a crooked grin she began to move towards the man who had according to his uniform been a cop in life and she held her shotgun ready level with the creature's rotten face. Three seconds later there was a deafening roar as the corridor was spattered with rotting flesh and brain matter. The result had been a little more brutal than she had expected as Shaznay wiped the spray back from her face, careful not to ingest any of the matter noticing at the same time that she had reached the staircase that she required. Suddenly it seemed that those two cowardly bastards leaving her might have been a blessing after all. She couldn't help but feel she would be fine on her own, just God help any fucking thing that tried to get in her way.

Daniel Shaw was dead. His grey features covered now by the coats and other random items of clothing that Paula and Robert had retrieved from the lost and found which was one of the few things that had survived thus far inside the theatre. There had been tears shed after they had tried to revive their friend but the attempts had been feeble and useless at best which they had known at the time. Neither of them were trained even in the slightest form of first aid and with someone as sick as Dan had been they had faced an impossible task in trying to bring him back from the dead. Even if they had managed this seemingly impossible task, they simply didn't possess the materials to keep him alive and stable but with the guilt that plagued them they had tried to resuscitate him non-the less. Paula had taken it especially badly, the death just adding to the feelings from abandoning Shaznay, which now seemed to have affected her mentally to almost the state of a complete breakdown. On numerous occasions she had begun rambling to herself, the babble making no sense whatsoever and continuing at times for over an hour until she either slept or wore herself out. During these babbling sessions she would become completely incoherent, ignoring Roberts's attempts to calm her or even in one instance to slap her out of it.

A day had now passed since they had made their pathetic escape attempt but for Robert it felt like fucking months already. At least before now the option of leaving was there but now they were simply trapped, what remained of this building had become their tomb and it was this thought that was beginning to eat away at him. The fact that he seemed to have lost the simple release of conversation wasn't helping things either, even when Paula was not talking rubbish she usually only responded to him by saying she was sorry or that she wanted to go home. It was fucked up and there was simply nothing he could do about it although he had at least found a new game that had kept him busy for the past hour or so. Sitting with the doors wide open his legs dangling into the abyss that had been created by what he could only assume had been a gas explosion Robert looked out onto the army of creatures that continued to do what they did. Continuously searching for mouthfuls of human flesh and it was this hunger that they had which was at least keeping him amused for now.

There were hundreds if not thousands of the fuckers that he could see filling the streets of Nottingham but those close to him were the ones that mattered in his little game. Every now and then one would spot him and instinct would bring their lumbering legs towards him, their deceased brains blind to the fact that there happened to be a gaping chasm between them and the living person they had fixed their sights on. There was of course only one result which was a freefalling zombie followed by the thud of flesh into rubble which was probably the nicest sound Rob had heard in a long time. It meant that with every sickening splat one more of those bastards had died or at least become eternally immobile which was certainly good enough for him. Thankfully he could also see through to the bottom of the pit allowing him to watch the bastards writhe around unable to pick their broken bodies back up again.

At least he had some form of satisfaction amid the mess although he knew that eventually even this new found novelty would probably wear thin. For now though he smiled as two fell at the same time, but he couldn't help the thoughts that tumbled through his mind, one of which reminding him that really he felt more alone that he had ever felt in his entire life. If only he had perhaps had the courage to stay with Shaznay and keep running but he knew it was too fucking late for that now, his one and only chance had gone and Shaznay was most likely dead thanks to him. Unless he found another escape route, which he doubted he would, he was stuck here with a corpse, a crazy lady and his thoughts that were in no way positive or even all that sane. Robert decided to watch another three zombies fall into the hole before going back to check on Paula. He was sure she wouldn't have gone far, if she had even moved at all, he just hoped that at some point she would snap out of this fucking state that she was in. He doubted that she would any time soon though, he was starting to doubt a lot of things worst of which was if he would ever get the chance to leave this theatre alive. Once again like the possibility of Paula's sanity returning he couldn't help but think it would never happen. He was fucked and he knew it.

As she awoke her first hazy instinct was fear as she scurried to her feet gripping the pistol tightly. The room came into focus and Shaznay instantly regained her composure as she recognised the cell in which she remained locked. After her encounter with the zombie although the canteen had been open and quite sufficiently stocked she had discovered to her dismay that the radio room had been inaccessible. Her attempts to pick the complicated lock had also proven a waste of time and energy. She had then begun hunting round for what seemed like hours, inspecting office after office and what seemed like a hundred bathrooms and closets until she had discovered a dead officer with a bundle of keys strapped to his hip. By this point the exhaustion of her run from the theatre had well and truly taken over and she had needed rest for which she had immediately known the safest possible place. She had passed back through the cells in order to reach the communications room and regardless of her will to try and radio for help sleep just had been the main necessity, she had struggled to keep her eyes from closing even as she had walked, the usual simplicity of putting one foot ahead of the other feeling like a monumental effort. Once in the room, she had simply drifted into unconscious bliss after mere seconds of enclosing herself in the lock up and had slept through the whole night until now which looking at the height of the sun had to be closing towards midday.

Shaznay simply sat for a moment allowing herself to wake up before checking she had all her things. She was pretty certain that the bundle of keys she had must contain the one that she sought and it was time to learn her fate. Despite the fact she knew that she might very soon be talking to someone who may be able to rescue her, Shaznay's hopes rose little if at all. With everything that had happened she knew that it would be foolish to get excited, after all it was a very strong possibility that everyone apart from herself was dead. Looking at the outside world it certainly didn't look good as far as the human race was concerned but she had to try, it was after all the only hope that she had. It was with this thought in mind that she unlocked the cell and began the short walk to her destination. God she hoped someone had stopped those fuckers before they had taken everything.

    She had seen her, it had to be, it couldn't be anyone else of that she was certain. She had never been more positive of anything in her life. A smile erupted on her face as she sprinted towards her; despite the distance between them her arms were already held out ready in anticipation of the loving warm embrace that she would receive. Her legs pumped as fast as they possibly could as tears of joy began to flow freely down her face, she was nearly there now. She had almost reached her happiness.
    As she came within five yards the smell hit her, it suddenly felt wrong and she realised almost immediately what she had done but it was too late. This woman was no longer her mother but she had wanted to believe it so badly that nothing else had mattered except the hug that she wanted so much. She had let her heart rule her head and for that she knew she must now pay the ultimate price, everything had changed in a heartbeat. Happiness to sadness, delight to fear and worst of all life to death. She tried to stop but she was too close and moving far too fast. Her trainers skidded on the mud as she crashed into the fence where the flailing arms that were waiting for her enveloped her body. There were more arms than her mother's, a lot more and within an instant she felt a searing pain all over as they began tearing into her flesh. As she tried to scream all that escaped was a liquid gargle, her windpipe had already been devoured by one of the hungry beasts and she felt the blackness quickly closing in around her. As she looked up she saw the twisted face that had once been the woman she had loved with every fibre of her being and she knew now for certain it was no longer her. The face that she saw before unconsciousness claimed her was that of pure evil and nothing more.
    It took two minutes for her to bleed to death but the feeding frenzy would continue for quite some time more on her remaining corpse, the

fresh blood attracting hundreds of the walking dead to the feast that had already begun.

"It may be that we have all lived before and died, and that this is hell"
    A.L Prusick

Chapter 9

Frank looked on at the sleeping forms of his three new companions smiling as he did so, for the first time in an age not actually feeling alone and angry. Nothing made up for the loss of his departed angel but for the first time since those fuckers had taken her from him he actually felt some other form of emotion apart from his burning rage that he knew had pretty much consumed his mind. Now though it suddenly seemed different, he had another cause to fight for apart from the simplicity of survival alone, three people with him to help keep each other's spirits high and most of all to help keep each other alive. It was certainly something to cling to and that was all that he needed to keep a smile on his face and a positive edge to his soul.

Camp had been set up in the cafeteria where they had laid down blankets that had been found in the janitor's closet, it was hardly a soft comfortable bed but it would certainly do. It was really the ideal place for them, being a large open space it would give them a head start should anything bad happen while they slept. Should any of those monsters manage to get inside they would see them coming a mile away which would give them plenty of time to run or at least prepare to defend themselves against an oncoming attack. Further safety precautions had also been taken after the group had eaten the previous night,

Frank and Sean had spent a good two hours using the flimsy tables to board up the windows as best they could, both men quite happy with what they had accomplished with the minimal supplies that they had possessed. For the simple fact that it was a school had meant that there had been little of any use for them to use for fortification. With what they had managed though, it would take a large group of the bastards to break through that was for certain which helped to keep the morale amongst the group quite high. Considering the giant heap of shit that could quite easily drag down their moods, the combination of finding new survivors and the fact they felt quite safe and secure was enough to overshadow the crap for now and keep things positive.

Garred glanced at the sleeping group again before rising slowly, his knees cracking with the laboured movement. His joints ached and he could feel the beginning of a headache gnawing at the base of his skull but these minor grievances bothered him little as he stretched towards the dingy cafeteria ceiling. He walked across the room, down the hall and towards the front door feeling the need for some fresh air to hopefully clear away the cobwebs of sleep.

Despite the fact he knew the air would be tainted with the smell of dead rotting flesh he hoped it would wake him a little and he just felt like a walk to try and counteract the headache he could feel. He would probably throw rocks at a few of the zombies while outside just to amuse himself which shouldn't be too much of a challenge judging on the noise he could hear through the closed double doors. The groaning seemed louder than he could remember and as he un-slid the two bolts and walked out into the fresh air it wasn't hard to see why it was so damn noisy. There were fucking hundreds of them surrounding every inch of the school. Not one centimetre of fence remained clear as the swarm seemed to ripple with movement. "Have the bastard things started multiplying?" Were Frank's words that he uttered to himself as the dumbfounded expression remained etched onto his frozen features, his gaze unable to shift from the sight before him. They were simply everywhere; it was the most frightening thing he had ever seen and he couldn't help but wonder where the fucking things had all come from. Normally the fuckers were quite spread out and certainly never massed together like this, it was almost as though they had been alerted to the presence of human flesh within the gates. Surely they hadn't grown more intelligent overnight, after all these things were fucking brain dead morons at best.

There had been no more than thirty or forty the last time he had been outside but now the size of the army had increased at least five fold, the group was simply too large for him to count. He was positive the zombies couldn't know anyone was inside, unless of course something or someone had managed to grab their attention and it was with this thought that his heart immediately jumped into his throat. He ran back inside, a nervous sweat spreading on his forehead as he prayed that she would be sleeping soundly. He tore back the blanket that he had assumed covered her completely and was immediately horrified to see that there were only some clothes and supplies underneath, no sign of the girl. She was gone. "Wake up! Rhianne is missing!" Frank screamed at the top of his voice not even knowing where to start searching for the poor little thing, feeling a massive urge to throw up the worry had hit him so hard. Despite what he wanted to believe he knew deep within that there would probably be only one outcome to this situation that had developed so suddenly. He quickly looked in the kitchen to find everything as they had left it and then sprinted back into the dining area to see the other two now standing and looking as startled as he had felt on pulling back her covers.

Without even saying anything all three ran from the room, Abbey and Sean taking the class rooms inside the building and Frank returning to the fresh air that he had moments ago tried to use in order to clear his headache. The fear and knowledge of what had probably occurred was horrifying as they all searched for Rhianne as fast as they could simply praying that she would turn up somewhere healthy and safe.

Sean tore through the first door he reached shouting her name at the top of his voice but to no avail, moments later he heard Abbeys voice from the next room on as she too prayed that she would receive an answer to her calls. The same synchronised search continued through the building until they had done a clear sweep of every room inside, both panting from their exertions as they headed outside praying that Frank had uncovered more than they had. What they saw as soon as they stepped outside told them everything that they needed to know as Abbey began to sob immediately, Sean jogging over to the other hysterical figure about a hundred yards to his left.

Frank was thrashing a crow bar through the fence at any zombie that was close enough to hit, tears staining his cheeks and screams of pain and sorrow escaping his mouth with every swing that he took. Every ounce of energy he had went into each strike and the closer that Sean got to him he knew that their worst nightmare had indeed come true.

What looked like gallons of blood stained the ground around where Frank stood and from the strong coppery smell in the air it confirmed that crimson mess was indeed fresh. Small chunks of flesh and bone littered the ground as it came closer into view making it almost impossible for Sean to control his own emotions especially when he saw the bloodstained ribbon that Rhianne had worn in her hair. All he wanted to do was join in and keep hitting the zombies until each last one of them were dead but he knew he had to fight the rage and torment that he now felt inside after all they were powerless against the masses of walking dead. He knew too that during moments of rage mistakes could be made and he had to ensure that despite this disaster those fucking things took no one else from the group. They were all at mental breaking point and were they to crack as a unit he knew it would certainly spell the end for them which was the last thing that they could afford, it was too fucking simple to die without making it easier for the flesh hungry bastards. He had to keep a strong head even though he felt more than ever that he had seen and taken enough of the surrounding bullshit.

As Frank lifted his arms back once more it felt as though his blood had turned to acid and his muscles had turned to lead but he knew he could keep swinging until the aching limbs fell off. He was crying for Rhianne, for Sharon the love of his life and for every single person that had been swallowed up by this never-ending pestilence. He hated it more that he thought it was even possible to hate something, with every living, breathing moment something else just seemed to appear or happen that made things even worse and make him hate these things that little bit more. He knew now that this hell would never be over, it just wouldn't stop until it had consumed everything around it, it was surely the end of mankind, he could simply see no other outcome. As he prepared to bring the crowbar down with force once again he felt a grip on his gore spattered arms, he knew without looking that it would be Sean and he knew that because of his efforts he would never be able to shake away the hold he had over him. Sean was more powerful that him and he was too tired from his labours to even thing about struggling against the hold. He reluctantly let the bar fall to the bloodstained ground and turned to the other man noticing that he too was crying, neither of them knew what to say or do it was just too fucked up a situation for either of them to react too. Frank just simply shook his head and let out a long breath wishing that there was something that any of them could do to change the horror that had happened while they had all slept.

"Let's go back inside and get you cleaned up." Were the only words that Sean could muster as he put his arm around him and began to walk back toward the school. As they slowly reached the building, Abbey forced a half smile at the two men but it was obvious that she wanted to give up and break down too, this death brought the memories of the loss of her own child flooding back more than ever but she was tough and determined as ever to stay strong as the trio made their way back inside to the cafeteria each and every one of them lost for words. Rather than cleaning up Frank made his was over to the large bag of supplies he had brought retrieving first a half bottle of scotch followed by an unopened one, which he threw to Sean with a forced smile etched on his face. "Make the most of it you two, these are all that's left." He said as he unscrewed the cap on his bottle and took a very large mouthful of the dark liquid.

Despite the fact that it was only early in the day the three of them began to drink and did so slowly through the rest of the day despite the fact that they were well aware that they should be more cautious for the fact there was an ever growing army of dead outside. The few ideas they had mustered for strengthening the building and fence outside would just have to wait though, it could be done tomorrow. They all needed some mental breathing space and they certainly fucking deserved one, they had witnessed and been through hell and on top of all this they had to accept that it would probably only get worse as time continued. They knew that unless they received help or found rescue, they were fighting a losing battle that could only result in their deaths.

Robert Angel was tired and seriously wound up as he begrudgingly ate a family size bag of skittles for his breakfast. His hopes that Paula's mental state would get better had taken a serious nosedive through the night as she had spent the hours of dark either screaming or crying to herself louder than he had thought possible. All attempts to calm her had proven pointless, as she had at one stage struck out at Robert, splitting his lip and bruising his cheek in the process. He had eventually given up his attempts and decided to dispose of the corpse that had once been his friend and work colleague instead. He had expected hysterics from Paula as he had dragged the lifeless form past her but surprisingly he got nothing, not even a sob.

Her glassy expression stayed the same and her ramblings continued uninterrupted which had thankfully made a difficult job that little bit easier for him. It had taken little thought on how to deal with the task as there were very limited possibilities for Robert to choose from. Keeping the cadaver in either the closet, the bathroom or the hall which were the only rooms left apart from the janitors office would mean that the stink would stay inside which was something he had not been too fond of, besides watching a friend rot didn't seem to appealing to him either. This left one of two choices, either out the front which was the twenty-foot drop onto the rubble of the theatre, or the back which was the massive drop into the gaping hole into the ground. It was the latter that he had decided on knowing that if he had chosen the front, the creatures would have been able to reach his friend and feed on his body. Robert accepted the fact that he was dead but no one deserved for that to happen to them even after their hearts had stopped beating.

He was sat at the front for the first time since the explosion as he crunched the last few skittles in the bag hating the sugary taste that he used to class as one of his favourite sweets. He thought of Daniel and the fact he couldn't face seeing his body at the bottom of the pit which made him question his own resolve even more that he already had. He knew that he would probably never look out of the back again unless he really had to now he had used that exit to dispose of his friend's body and this made him feel utterly cowardly and weak.

As a zombie struggled to drag its broken body across the rubble below him, he gritted his teeth as he heard another loud wail from inside. Despite the fact that he was only feet away from another human he had never felt so alone in his life and he was running out of ideas on how he could change this situation that for him just seemed to be growing worse. He didn't hate Paula for having this mental breakdown, he hated her for pulling him back towards the theatre and most of all he hated his cowardly self for following her and listening. Despite this though he knew he had to do something though, to try everything he could to snap her out of this and then to maybe even come up with another escape plan although that could wait, for one he doubted they could even get out of the building let alone find rescue or safety elsewhere. He let the empty sweet packet go and watched it spiral to the floor and land next to one of many dead creatures. As another sob erupted from the room behind he stood with a long sigh. He would try once again to gain some sanity from his friend and if he failed once more he had no idea what the hell he would do, God he felt so fucking alone. Frighteningly the thought of joining Daniel's body in the deep hole flashed through his mind as he made his way inside once again.

Chapter 10

Her heart was racing and her breathing laboured but for once it was through excitement rather than through the exertion of running away from those fucking zombies. The radio control room was now open thanks to the key bundle that she had now fastened back to her belt and the excitement of what she was about to attempt was taking over her actions and the control of her body. She took a long drink of the water she had retrieved from the canteen and also let the last piece of her chocolate fall to the floor. She had eaten enough to see her through for a few hours and the fact that she could be moments away from human contact that could lead to her rescue meant for definite that nourishment could wait.

She looked at all the dials, before her were so many buttons and screens that she could only begin to imagine where to start but for one thing she was glad the thing was all lit up and seemed to be working ok. She could hear the slight hiss of static and could see three separate hand and headsets that could be used of which she chose the closest to her merely for convenience rather than any intelligent decision. She placed the headphones on and pressed the hand set before stating simply "Hello." She waited anxiously, hoping beyond all hope that she would receive an answer as the seconds ticked agonizingly by, various thoughts concerning rescue and human contact tumbling rapidly through her head. She had no idea if she was using the machine correctly or if it was on the right frequency but she would leave the dials as they were, she just hoped that they remained in the correct position from the last time they were in use. "Can anyone hear me?" She said, this time with a little more power and volume in her voice, still knowing that there would probably be no answer to her question, after all the simple notion of other survivors existing seemed quite farfetched considering the state of the outside world. She carried on asking the same questions though for over an hour before she accepted that no one would answer on the set frequency and began to fiddle with the many dials hoping that she would stumble on something although it would certainly be by luck rather than judgement. Her hopes were certainly low but Shaznay's determination remained strong as she continued with her efforts despite the demoralizing silence that greeted her every attempt.

It took an age of searching before she finally found something apart from the hiss of static but it served to be a stupid government radio broadcast that had been put on a loop telling everyone to remain indoors and wait for the situation to be dealt with by the professionals. As she chuckled to herself on hearing the statement another noise tore through the air almost stopping her heart instantly in the process. Unfortunately it had not been the sound of survivors or even anything at all from the radio like she had hoped to hear. It was like something she had never heard before, zombie like but different, it sounded more evil, louder and for certain more frightening than the usual groans that escaped those things. She gripped her weapon tightly and pressed a large switch on the communications console, which she correctly assumed was the power button. As she tried to rise again the noise erupted from within the building once more only this time she knew it was louder and that it had certainly moved closer. Her feet were rooted to the spot and she felt her body begin to tremble, she had never been so scared in her life and she knew that soon she would come face to face with whatever this thing was, she just hoped that its bark was worse than its bite and if not, that she had enough firepower to deal with it.

She was a mess that was for sure and she was fucking angry. Paula would not respond coherently to any of his attempts to talk or reason with her. It had become a fucking useless task even trying to get any sort of response from her never mind a sane one.

"Its all our fault, were going to die here." Were the only things she would now say, repeating them over and over so rapidly her breathing had become laboured and her hair matted with sweat. Usually a calm rational person, Robert had accepted the fact that he had lost the will to help her; he didn't have the patience or the energy to try and get her back to who she was if that was indeed possible. He had accepted the fact that she had completely lost the plot, which he knew, was something he was powerless to fix. Christ he couldn't blame her for losing her marbles though, he was quite surprised that he still held onto his sanity looking at the grand scheme of things but that didn't make the current situation any easier for him to cope with. The constant barrage of noise that came from her was grinding away at him and he could feel it grating on his nerves, he had even started pacing about and started singing to himself in an effort to drown it out but it was having very little effect.

Growing unsure of how long he could tolerate the torment he was feeling he had now decided to take a place back outside amongst the living dead bizarrely hoping that the noise of a thousand groans would be easier to hear than the ramblings of a mad woman. He just had to contend with the fact that his dead friend was of course visible every time his eyes wandered into the cavern below. He had known of course that he was wrong and it would be no better outside but he had to try, it was becoming too much for him to take watching and listening the madness inside. He could feel himself beginning to break and the mere thought of this scared him more than anything had so far. At least until now he had kept his self-control but this too like Paula's sanity was slipping further and further away.

She had left the communications room, everything had become deathly silent as she moved forward so cautiously it seemed she moved in slow motion. Shaznay had no idea what the fuck had made that noise but she didn't want to confront it if possible although she doubted she would be that fortunate. After all she wanted to remain here at the station for as long as possible which pretty much meant avoiding this thing would be an impossibility. Her plan was simply to make it back to the cell and lock herself in knowing that whatever the hell it was, it wouldn't be able to make it through the bars, she could then at least shoot at the bastard from a safe place or so she at least hoped. She had removed the cell key from the bundle and gripped it ready along with her shotgun, more than anything she would at least be prepared should she have to face this thing before she made it to safety. Should she need to make a sprint for it too, the last thing she wanted was to die because she couldn't lock a bloody door in time.

Her tiptoes took her around the first kink in the long haul and thankfully it was clear as she breathed a long sigh of relief despite the fact she knew that she was still far from her goal. Her hands were sweaty and her knees weak as she continued as silently as she could be with her steady progress. She knew there was one more corner and a set of doors to get to where she wanted to be and the temptation to sprint was overwhelming until her ears suddenly picked up on something. She froze immediately listening intently wondering if it had been the wind outside or the thing that she so wanted to avoid but she knew that it was most likely the latter, she wasn't expecting this cruel new world to throw any favours her way. "What the fuck." She whispered as she heard it once again, a dull thud although this time it continued, every second it came again: thud, thud, thud and with each one, the noise was growing louder.

It took less than ten seconds for her to realize that these noises were coming from behind her and a few seconds more for her to realise that these thuds were indeed footsteps. As she turned she knew in her frantically beating heart that whatever it was, it would be there and indeed she was right. It was one of the dead but it was like nothing she had seen since this hell had taken over. This creature must have been a gargantuan man in life, at least seven feet tall and eighteen stone in weight and as he let out another deafening scream she knew that she had to react immediately hoping and praying that this thing could be dealt with in the same way as the others. She swung the shotgun over her back knowing that the distance between the two of them was too great for it to be affective and withdrew the handgun that she had already loaded. Shaznay steadied her hand and shouted the words "fuck you" before squeezing the trigger knowing that she could outrun this thing but feeling the urge to stop it instead. She had never felt the fear that surged through her veins as she continued to rapidly press the trigger as fast as her shaking fingers would allow even after the first two bullets hit home. The first bullet hit the giant on the left collarbone, flesh and muscle tissue erupting into the air like a geyser. Within the blink of an eye the second missile followed although this one was much more devastating, taking out the eye socket with a sickening crunch as a large portion of skull and brain matter exploded into the wall behind. The following few shots whipped only inches past the flailing zombie before three consecutive missiles once again found their mark. Each deadly shot tore through a portion of the dead man's face leaving behind only complete brutal carnage.

Shaznay eventually stopped her firing, a bead of sweat falling from the tip of her nose onto the pistol, dissolving almost instantly with a hiss from the heat of the weapon. The smell of cordite burned her nostrils as she panted heavily watching the bizarre scene unfold slowly before her. The zombie teetered for what seemed like an eternity, the pulped excuse for a head threatening to fall to the ground before the giant finally toppled with a deafening crack. As a giant dust cloud lifted around the fallen figure she watched intently knowing and not daring to let down her guard, anything could fucking happen and she was going to be ready for whatever could still occur.

He looked at her and then down at his hands, tears streaming freely down his face as he sobbed loudly unable to comprehend what he had just done. He had already tried to convince himself that his actions had been rational, just a cause of his surroundings but he knew that there was no excuse. Yet again his actions spoke louder than any words ever could, like leaving Shaznay amongst the monsters he had once again carried out an unforgivable act. He felt despicable, he was a filthy fucking murderer and now he realised he had no one and nothing but himself to blame. Not only that there was the sickening guilt that not only had he just killed someone but he had murdered his last remaining friend.

After spending another two hours outside, still able to hear Abbeys ranting and screaming he had finally snapped. He had felt his rage rising and had been unable to control the evil feelings within, it had simply become too much for him to take. Robert had taken a piece of rubble the size of a cricket ball and led by pure rage and frustration he had sprinted inside shouting at her to shut up. Consumed by her breakdown, Abbey had of course not responded which led to his actions, which now caused him to empty his stomach contents on the ground next to her unmoving body. He had hit her so many times, the blood still covered his wrists and hands and the ground all around him but even worse he could see pieces of her hair and skull stuck to the makeshift weapon he had used.

The tears simply wouldn't stop, even as he stood and tried to calm his almost hyperventilated breathing there was no end to it. He knew why, he wasn't naïve enough to think he could just shake away these feelings that were so intense he just couldn't take them. Despite the fact he had already vomited he still felt nauseous and despite the fact he was frightened he knew exactly what he had to do, he had no other choice. Robert led himself shakily back outside, glancing back as he reached the door and whispering an apology to his newly deceased friend. As the fresh air once more blasted his face he didn't even allow himself to consider what he was doing as he took one-step forward and allowed gravity to take over. Robert simply fell into the abyss, his tears still streaming in the few moments that were left of his life, he knew after what he had done only hell could await him but that was still surely better than the guilt that he felt. The last thought he had before his skull shattered on the rubble below was the fact that the fucking zombies had finally gotten to him, maybe not directly but they had still caused all of this. The fucking things had won.

"The evil that men do lives after them, the good is oft interred with their bones."
W. Shakespeare

Chapter 11

He could hear the sounds but through his grogginess he was unsure if it was a dream as he struggled to shake of the slumber that seemed unwilling to let him go. Sean blinked rapidly trying to speed things up as he sat slowly feeling a slight sickness in his stomach as he did so. With the rancid taste in his mouth, it did not take him long to remember the whiskey and as the noises became a little clearer a feeling of utter terror soon took over as he shouted for the other two to wake up, not even knowing if they still lay next to him. As it were they did and they heard his croaky cry, both sitting upright also fighting the same struggle to clear their hung over vision as the terrifying sounds invaded their senses along with the slumbered minds that gripped each of them in their waking moments.

The banging and scratching could be heard all around them and the usual chorus of groans seemed once again much louder that it had done the night before, it immediately told them all one simple terrifying thing. They knew without hesitation that the fuckers were inside the school grounds and they knew that if they had just strengthened the perimeter the night before then they would have probably woken under different circumstances but it seemed there was little time to dwell on their mighty fuck up. Even in the most messed up of situations like they had faced, they had known that safety should have come first but they had let the tragedy that had occurred take over their actions. They had risked their lives and now they would have to deal with the consequences, plain and simple.

"Shit, what do we do?" Were Abbeys words as she looked at the shaking barricades that were struggling to hold back the army of dead that were now almost within touching distance. Neither man had an answer for her though; Sean briefly made eye contact and just shrugged although the worry in his eyes was clearly visible as he took the pistol from his belt and loaded a round ready for what seemed would be a pending attack. His two companions soon followed this example as they steadied themselves for whatever danger they were sure would be waiting around almost any corner they turned. It was quite obvious to each of them that should the barricades give way that it would be the end for them, there were simply too many of the bastard things as they had seen for themselves the night before and not only this there were quite a few doors and ground level windows that would allow the fuckers an easy access to the inside. Suddenly it seemed what had been such a safe place for them had now become more dangerous than they could have ever thought possible. In the space of a day yet again for the three survivors all hell had broken loose.

"We have to try and get back to the sewers, we have come further than the crash site so it should at least be safe down there." Sean stated, knowing that logically this plan would be accepted by the other two, he could see no other possible plan for them. Staying inside the building, which was majorly compromised, was as simple as committing suicide and they all knew that the streets were littered with the fucking things especially since Rhianne's unfortunate demise had attracted hordes of the bastards to the vicinity. The thought quickly crossed Franks mind to suggest returning to his house although after the incident in his kitchen he knew that it wasn't strong enough to last for a long time and besides there was probably no way of even making it back to the front gate of the school never mind all the way up the street.

After quickly ensuring the dining hall and the kitchen were clear the three of them moved towards the door leading out into the hallway and classrooms. They had no idea where the nearest sewer entrance was or how the fuck they would get outside so one step at a time was the only way forward for the trio as they wondered how on earth they would ever survive what seemed like an impossible situation. Frank pressed his hand to the door first followed by his ear, the drumming and groaning from the boarded window next to him so loud it drowned out any chance of him being able to hear through the wooden surface. He concentrated hard and remained unmoving for over a minute before he turned and smiled slightly at his two new friends. "I think were safe guys." He said, a sound of relief in his statement as he placed his hand on the knob and turned it slowly, cautious to make as little noise as possible although from the racket outside he wondered momentarily why he bothered. He listened once again as the door opened a crack and he was greeted with the silence that he had hoped for although with the surrounding wails he knew not to take anything for granted. He cautiously stepped out into the hall with his gun at the ready, the other two close behind him. Thankfully, as he had hoped, the large main door had thankfully held firm against the figures outside. He could hear more sounds to his right though, which presumably came from the classrooms leaving their hopes of escaping in that direction slightly dented. They had closed all of the doors after their initial inspection on arrival at the building, which now seemed to be proving a good form of safety, as the hallway remained thankfully zombie free. Luckily the fucking things were too damn stupid to open doors which was probably the only reason that the three of them hadn't been killed in their sleep so at least they could be happy for this small mercy.

"Let's head to the back of the building to see if we can find an empty room to look out of. We need to find a sewer grate or anyway to get out of this place." Abbey spoke from the back of the small group, happy when the two men nodded their agreement without actually turning to face her. She knew that they had to find a way underground otherwise they would surely die and it was this thought that made her hands begin to tremble as she walked, the fear of her life coming to an end affecting her more than ever now the possibility seemed so imminent. Despite her fear though she knew that they at least had a small chance, they had all survived this far and come through so many horrors, which told her that they at least stood a fight at getting through this newest mess although her doubts now massively outweighed any confidence that she had felt.

As they began walking and passed the first two opposing doors it was clear without even checking that the zombies had gained entry within. The groaning could clearly be heard as could the clattering of furniture as one of the beasts presumably tripped within the confines of the room. The next set proved the same although Abbey spent a few seconds with her ear pressed against one door before she heard the distinct sounds of the groaning undead within. It was only as the group reached the third set of classrooms that they heard the hopeful silence that they sought so dearly. Sean stood at one door and Frank at the other waiting intently, hoping and praying that the quiet would continue and for both of them it thankfully did. They listened for an age, until they were certain it would be safe before they finally and reluctantly made a move, Sean stating that they should try his door first, it would after all be facing the back fence which was where they hoped to find the fewest zombies and hopefully a way out. Should this area also be thickly infested then they had no backup plan how to escape meaning that for now it was a fingers crossed moment. The rear of the school being clear was simply based on the assumption that the fuckers had gained entry to the front although they could in no way be certain what horrors awaited outside regardless of how the zombies had entered the compound.

As Sean finally gripped the handle with his sweaty palm, his heart begun to beat rapidly in his chest, the usually simple action taking all the courage that he could muster. God he hoped the room was empty and even more so he hoped for an escape as he pulled downwards with his hand and slowly pushed the door inwards cursing as the hinges creaked. After one look, he breathed out heavily as he saw the emptiness greet him, nothing nasty was waiting and thankfully there was no need to fight. It seemed they were safe for the time being although the hard part was still to come, which was a fact, that none of them could possibly forget.

He motioned for his friends to follow him into the room as he made his way towards the window, which surprisingly didn't have an army of zombies on the other side, so far so good at least he thought as he approached the glass. It was only as he was able to look outside that he realised why and also how much of a lucky advantage they had stumbled upon. The slope that ran down from their new vantage point was only twenty feet long before it reached the flat surface of the playground but it was certainly enough, it was very steep which meant what would be a struggle for a person proved to be an impossibility for the zombie's to climb. The trio stood in awe, amazed by this piece of fortune as they looked on at the figures stumbling around below, unable to help the dumbfounded grin that each of them wore amazed at the sight before them and at the luck that they had received.

"Well fuck me, can you believe that." Frank was the first to speak as he shook his head slowly from side to side.

"About time we got a bit of fortune though." Abbey replied almost chuckling as she saw one of the monsters fall over in its attempt to scale the hill.

Sean meanwhile had begun searching for the next part of their escape, although happy at this piece of luck he knew that the bastards could still get to them somehow and he wasn't about to risk anything. He was more aware than ever that there were hundreds of the cunts pressing up against the barricades at the front of the building, which could of course give way at any time. He would be prepared though as he searched for anything that would jump out at him in order to aid their escape. Thankfully it only took a few scans of the grounds outside to see what he wanted as Sean began waving for the other two to join him, a grate lay by the fence and thankfully for them it was one of the smaller ones that were a damn sight easier to move. Despite his strength and the addition of his two companions, without a crowbar they would never have shifted one of the larger sewer entrances but once more luck seemed to favour them for which they could only be overjoyed. As the other two joined him and saw what he had found they certainly shared his happiness although the discovery came with a large sense of concern too looking at what stood between them and this newly found goal.

"There's at least a hundred of them out there though, what are we going to do?" Abbey's words filled the silence but neither of the men answered her question for what seemed like an absolute age, their minds contemplating all available options. After all it was three of them against a hundred or more flesh hungry zombies, which seemed like a fucking impossibility albeit one that they would soon have to face regardless of the risk. As no one seemed able to answer the question that Abbey had asked, the three of them simultaneously began scanning the room for anything that would help them reach their target knowing that ideas or not they simply had to make an escape. The pistols that they had were only useful to stop a handful of the fuckers at most but for the mass that waited outside they would prove pretty useless in the grand scheme of things. It was after a few minutes of useless searching that Abbey walked over to one of the long tables and simply kicked it over, the two men assuming that it was out of frustration and fear rather than anything else. It was only as she picked one end up and motioned for them to grab the rest that they knew what she wanted to do, it was the perfect barricade for them to barge past the fuckers. After all the balance of a zombie was pretty much non-existent, so despite the plans simplicity it seemed Abbey could have found the perfect solution but of course they knew there would only be one sure way to find out.

Chapter 12

The fucker hadn't moved, she had stood there for what must have been fifteen minutes waiting for anything, any sign of life but the giant had remained still and thankfully completely void of any movement. It was only after she was completely sure, Shaznay had approached the demon, replaced her pistol with the shotgun, which she had then held firmly against what remained of the creatures head. So much fury had burned within her as she had looked down upon this thing, a pure hatred for it and all its kind making her tremble with sheer emotion.

She had screamed once more as she pulled the trigger, the kickback of the weapon threatening to rip her arm from the socket as she felt the resulting gore spatter her legs and lower abdomen although this had bothered her little at the time. It was only then, as she looked down at the headless figure that she was happy. Happy and satisfied that this thing would no longer be a threat; she knew she had killed it although she equally accepted that she could not rest despite the tiredness that seemed to sweep over her thanks to the adrenaline dump that her body had received. She just had to make sure there were no more zombies hiding away within the station, she doubted there would be any the size of this one lurking about but she had to check to ensure her safety. After all by the looks of things every other poor bastard that had tried to survive within the station had obviously met their demise but not her, Shaznay was more determined than ever to stay alive and she would not let one of these maggot-ridden bastards grab her unaware. She took a quick look back at the communications room, the urge to continue her contact attempts were still strong but she knew safety would have to come first and with that thought she begrudgingly set off on her way. After a few steps despite her lack of energy and will a smile spread across her pretty face, for the first time Shaznay realised that it was time for her to hunt them.

Over half an hour of searching room after room and she had found only one zombie, a legless freak crawling about in one of the bathrooms posing very little threat to her. It had been a grotesque sight though; the creature that had once been a woman, obviously ravaged by the other zombies before she had died. Bite marks covered what was left of her naked body, которая had already begun to seriously rot, pieces of flesh had fallen from her with every movement making the sight even more unbearable to take.

Shaznay had given the corpse exactly the same shotgun treatment that the giant had received before then ensuring that the room was in no way compromised for the demons to gain access from the outside. She had been happy that it was safe and had continued her relentless search that had so far turned up very little apart from the occasional dead policeman or woman although no more infected were discovered. Her energy was seriously lagging too, each step that she took combined with the concentration that was needed to hear every noise was taking its toll as she stopped and rested her head against the corridor wall exhaling deeply as she did so. After her long sigh and a quick glance at the map she estimated there were maybe another six or so rooms for her to look in but she couldn't get through them all with the way that she was feeling despite how much she wanted the task to be over with. Even though she had rested once since the escape from the theatre she had endured so much her body seemingly had nothing left to give apart from a need to recuperate. As much as her strong will wanted to continue though she knew there was only one form of action which was simply to sleep so that she could face everything once again with a fresh mind. She knew that as fucked up as the situation was, she would need her energy to face whatever hurdles came her way and with this thought she made her way slowly back to the canteen.

She would grab some food and drink before going to rest once again although this time she had decided to sleep in the communications room with the radio on. She doubted very much that she would receive any form of transmission but some hope still remained however little it was. She knew that within this room she would also be quite safe so long as she kept the door shut and locked, after all the creatures weren't that smart.

A bowl of beans were the dish of the day that she happily spooned through, enjoying every morsel that slid down her throat. After the absolute garbage she had been forced to consume while trapped at the theatre, this usually simple meal was now absolute bliss. Alongside this Shaznay happily sipped at her cup of black coffee equally loving the taste that this hot drink brought. The caffeine would certainly not keep her from resting though; no amount of stimulants could keep away the sleepiness that she now felt.

The kettle at the theatre had been broken which meant for the first few weeks they had the pleasure of a variety of fizzy drinks followed by tap water, which had grown very tiring and repetitive. She couldn't help think how suddenly the world had turned upside down and that things she had never really thought were important had suddenly become a massive luxury in her life. She smiled slightly as she rose from her cross-legged position on the floor, no need to do the dishes she thought as she stretched her tired body. She was ready to sleep and happy that she felt almost safe enough to do so, she knew that there were rooms she had yet to search but any zombies within would surely remain there until she had the energy to blow their fucking brains out. She had even decided that a shower would be her treat first thing after waking once more; it had been a fucking age since she had washed properly and although there was no one but herself to do this for she felt absolutely disgusting. As she looked down at her body, the blood and dirt stains made her want to wash even more and despite the fact she was so tired she changed her mind about sleep and headed to the changing rooms first. The food and drink had actually woken her somewhat, which meant for now her rest could be postponed for another short while at least.

She had checked the rooms carefully to ensure no monsters were lurking within, these were after all some of the unexplored rooms within the building. The gents had turned up nothing and neither had the ladies apart from a pair of clean jeans and underwear that she would happily take rather than her own tattered clothing. She now stood under the jets of ice-cold water, her skin covered in goose bumps and her nipples hardened due to the low temperature of the jet streams. She didn't care though, a hot shower would have been nicer but just to feel her naked body being cleaned was amazing in its self. She had lathered herself three times with the shower gel she had discovered and washed her hair twice, looking at her hands and how wrinkled they were becoming she knew she had been under the water for quite some time, cherishing the feeling that was another thing that she would normally take with a pinch of salt. With a happier sigh than what she was used to she finally turned the taps and walked back to where she had placed her clothes. As she took a seat on the long bench she admired her reflection in the mirror, impressed that despite her shocking diet she still kept the body that most women would kill for. The few bruises and the bad cuts on her face could go a miss but apart from that now she was clean she looked pretty damn good to say the world was collapsing around her.

Shaznay had been unable to locate a towel so she slid her wet thighs slowly into the silky knickers she had found, they fit pretty well for which she was thankful and as she grabbed for the jeans a crashing noise erupted from what had to be the room to her left. She froze instantly dropping the trousers; the only noise her breath as she waited for it to sound again. Agonizing seconds passed as she picked up the shotgun making her way through the door behind her and out into the hall, not caring that apart from the panties she wore she was completely naked. As she approached the door from which she assumed the noise had come Shaznay prayed that there weren't many of the fuckers hiding within and with a deep breath she pushed the door as hard as she could. As it flung open the stench hit her hard as she reeled back feeling a sickness instantly take over, it was only a tiny broom closet inside which someone had obviously used as a trap, pushing this creature within which she now prepared to kill. The badly decayed zombie groaned before lunging at her only to feel the wrath of an accurately placed shell milliseconds later.

Brain tissue spattered the ceiling as the zombie flew back and instantly hit the deck, Shaznay quickly sidestepping to avoid becoming covered in gore once again. She cursed a little as she did so, the hot metal of the fired weapon touching her naked breast and burning the skin slightly with a hiss. Se cursed the minor injury and looked on at the creature for a few seconds, once again to ensure it was dead. Thanks to the devastating nature of her weapon, it was which meant Shaznay could make her way back to the shower room realising for what must have been the umpteenth time again how tired she was. It seemed that this barrage of shit was certainly never ending.

It took Shaznay another five minutes in the shower room to get dressed; wearing her new jeans along with the bulletproof vest she felt the best and cleanest she had for a long time. Clean body, clean mind she had thought as she had tied her hair into a ponytail enjoying the cleanly washed smell as she did so. Despite her need to sleep she had begrudgingly taken an extra ten minutes to check the remaining rooms in the station, which to her delight were monster free. On a first glance though they didn't really turn up much of any use either, most of which had been only small offices although she had made a mental note to search them more thoroughly when she had more energy despite the fact that they had quite obviously been raided on a previous occasion. Finally she had gone back to the communications room, turned the machine on and issued a few unanswered maydays before curling up and finally giving in to the tiredness that she felt. Once again she was asleep within thirty seconds.

Chapter 13

The fear that they felt was unreal, so powerful but they knew regardless of this it was the only way to get to their goal, they had no other realistic choice. The only other option was to wait inside for the bastards to break in and get them, which they had accepted would not take that long and certainly didn't even merit consideration. They had decided that it was time for them to move as one by one they stepped out of the window with their makeshift barricade, careful not to slip on the steep decline outside. As they cautiously navigated their way down the slope they noticed after mere seconds that some of the corpses had already seen them; it was obvious that the longer they waited and the slower they moved the harder their task would become.

"On three we charge the bastards." Frank said, looking across to see the other two nodding in agreement and thankfully they wore the same look of horror on their faces that he assumed he also carried. His legs felt non-existent and sweat dripped from his chin, he was fucking terrified and not ashamed of this emotion in any way. He could feel the table shaking rapidly, unsure whether it was him or one of the others he began to count knowing that it could be the last things he ever said out loud. As he reached three the trio bolted, thankfully the action immediately having the desired effect as the first group of undead were sent hurtling easily to the ground around them. A rotted arm spiralled skywards as Sean screamed for them not to stop, their pace and power increasing as they continued to mow down any of the creatures that got in their way trampling hastily over the bodies that fell beneath them whilst trying to avoid the threat of being bitten from below.

As more of the demons toppled they knew they were getting closer to their goal and they could almost taste the freedom that lie waiting in the sewers below, there were just a few more zombies to get through and they had made it.

It took another five toppled corpses before they reached the entrance at which point the three of them discarded the temporary blockade and set to their own pre-discussed tasks working as fast as they humanly could. As Frank and Abbey began working to free the heavy slab of metal Sean was on point to try and stop any oncoming attackers as he took instant aim and fired into the skull of an approaching creature. A slice of matted hair flew into the air along with a shower of crimson as the monster dropped to the ground as he continued firing into the scattered mass of the enemy.

Thankfully he had sufficient time to pick his shots although the mob had by now all begun heading in their direction that made everything he did feel insanely rushed and pressurised. As he rapidly pumped the trigger another three times in quick succession, each bullet finding its intended target he heard the grinding of metal on concrete, his instincts immediately making him turn to see if they had managed to indeed free the grate. As he focussed on his friends, Abbey began shouting for him to come on as he simultaneously saw the horror emerge on Frank's face. Within the moment it had taken for him to turn and realise something was massively wrong he felt the burning pain erupt in his right ankle.

The shock more that the pain made him scream out loud as the realisation hit home as to what had occurred. Before he looked down he knew the reason behind the sharp jolt of agony and his thoughts were confirmed as he locked sights on the bastard that had just effectively ended his life. He heard Abbey scream as she had obviously witnessed what had just occurred and as he watched the fucker begin to chew the piece of his leg that it had ripped free he angrily jammed a fresh mag into his pistol feeling a tear run down his cheek as he did so. He shot the first bullet straight ahead taking out the closest of the oncoming mass as his frustration and desperation grew. "You dumb fuck!" He shouted as loud as he could unable to believe that he had been so fucking careless as his gaze shifted back to the zombie beneath him that was still busy eating the mouthful of flesh it had taken from him. With gritted teeth he pointed the weapon down rapidly pulling the trigger four times as he watched the bullets obliterate the creature's skull but knowing this hardly made up for what had just occurred. He knew his shots had been enough to kill the fucker that had bit him but he wasn't quite finished yet as he heard Franks voice shouting for him to hurry up and join them. By the echo he assumed they had already begun their decent and it was understandable why, the main bulk of the zombie mass were fucking close and they were simply fucking everywhere he looked but that mattered little now, in fact nothing mattered anymore. In the blink of an eye his journey had ended, he couldn't believe he had battled through so much to let a moment of carelessness take it all away from him. Sean took two more accurate shots into the oncoming crowd, the first hitting a woman in the throat and the second destroying the eye socket of the zombie next to her. It was the next shot that he turned on himself a second tear running down his cheek as he felt the hot nozzle of the gun burn into the underneath of his chin. As he increased the pressure on the trigger he heard Abbey's voice screaming once again before there was only darkness and for Sean Ryes. Suddenly the whole mess of shit was over.

    Sean had been dead before his body had hit the ground and thankfully Frank had dragged her below before the bastards had started feeding on him but still this did not make it any easier to accept that they had lost yet another survivor and friend. Abbey stood knee deep in the murky water sobbing as she heard Frank hurriedly sliding the grate back into place above, the groans becoming quieter and the visibility becoming limited as he did so. She didn't care that she was back below the ground once again wading amongst gallons of excrement it just didn't fucking matter anymore, yet another one had died and they had been unable to stop it from happening. She couldn't believe she had lost someone else, it seemed that everything would continue this way until either she was taken or she was left completely alone, they were down to just two now and the way things were going the number would just continue to decrease until there was no one left.

    Everything suddenly seemed so much more useless than it ever had, what was the point of even trying were her thoughts as she felt Franks arms slide around her shoulders in a warm embrace that she needed more than anything to stop her from giving up on her survival and really losing all hope. She cried heavily, all her pain and suffering rushing out and escaping for what was the first time since everything had begun, she could even feel Frank crying too knowing well that he like herself would have lost so much throughout this whole nightmare. Neither of them needed to speak as their embrace continued both of them just needing the release that only tears could bring as they realised they now only had one another to rely on. They needed the emotional discharge so that they could continue forwards and they needed it so that they could grieve albeit for this short moment in time but most of all they needed it for their sanity to remain intact.

A little over ten minutes later they had begun wading back in the direction that they had planned, not really caring for the time being where it would lead them. They were happy to be safe and that would do for now. They had also managed to quell their emotions, the tearful ten minutes seeming to have revived the two as much as humanly possible to say that they had just seen their compatriot blow out his own brains. They had briefly discussed Sean's death but had agreed that the less said the better, the same went with the unfortunate death of Rhianne that was also very fresh in their minds. There had been nothing that either of them could have done certainly when it came to Sean and if he hadn't ended his own life then he would have become one of those things eventually meaning they would have had to shoot him anyway. Either way they had to accept that even without the suicide he had been as good as dead which was how they had finished the conversation about him.

Thankfully they had packed torches to illuminate their way along the murky sewers without which they would have been left almost completely blind and helpless within the tunnels. They had lost the rations and blankets that Sean had carried but they still thankfully had two bags of supplies, which for now would have to do until they could hopefully discover more. They had included food, water and ammo, which they could at least be somewhat thankful for; after all without these vital items their survival would be impossible.

Not much had been discussed about a way forward as the choices for them were self-explanatory. There was only one logical plan for them to follow which would be to check the surface every time they had covered a reasonable amount of ground. They were both happy with this option but more so they just wanted to stay away from any form of danger for as long as possible meaning that the sewers were fine for the foreseeable future. As they continued their trek Abbey took a hold of Franks hand, not at all in any way meant than for comfort, which he himself knew but enjoyed the feel of her touch none the less. The small pleasure and warmth that it brought was something that they both needed badly right now.

    Three hours of heavy wading had passed before they agreed to check the surface above. Neither really wanting to but both Abbey and Frank knowing that they had little other choice. Both of them were hungry and tired and there was no possible way for them to sleep in their present location. The idea of eating amongst a river of human shit had not appealed to them either meaning that they now stood looking up at the manhole that seemed the only way for them to go. Strangely no groans could be heard from above but they were not about to take this for granted, they knew better than anyone that a positive seeming situation could soon turn round and fuck you over in a million different ways.

    Frank had decided to take the lead, clambering slowly up the eight rungs that protruded from the damp moss covered wall. He had insisted that Abbey remain below, knowing that if anything were lurking near enough to the cover above that he was certainly fucked if he didn't react quickly enough. He didn't want to get bitten that was for sure but he certainly didn't want to watch something happen to Abbey, which was why he had been so insistent that she stay down below while he checked out the surface. He knew that he would always blame himself partially for what had happened to his partner but as he felt his emotions begin to rise he knew there was certainly no time to dwell on these pains right now as he reached the metal disc above him.

    She watched anxiously as Frank shifted the heavy object, seeming to use every ounce of strength he had just to move it enough so that he could grab a proper hold. It was with a grunt he had pulled the grate to one side and had immediately taken one more step up and had peered cautiously out. Abbey gritted her teeth knowing that anything could happen to him in the vulnerable situation he was in but as he continued to climb to the surface her heart rate calmed a little hoping that everything was going to be all right. The urge to follow him was huge but she knew that he had been right in his instructions; he would quickly scout above before coming back for her although this meant an agonising wait alone in the sewer. She knew that anything could happen to him while he was alone but in the short time she had known him, she had seen that he could handle himself and that would have to be enough until she was with him once again which to be fair couldn't come soon enough. Each second seemed that ticked by seemed like an hour, her ears straining for any sounds but to her annoyance all she could hear were the drips of water in the murky tunnel. Her eyes never shifted from the sewer opening above as she waited patiently growing more and more worried until she finally heard the noise that she had been praying for.

"It's safe, and its good news Abbey. Come up." Frank's voice sounded full of promise and joy, which brought an instant smile to her previously concerned face as she hurriedly began climbing to the surface, her foot almost missing a step in her haste to see what he had found and also ensure he was ok. As she took his hand and gained her footing on dry ground her first surprise was that they were indoors, she had expected fresh air, a street and at least some zombies within eyeshot but none of the horror she had expected lie in waiting. As she brushed some of the filth from her shirt she looked around noticing two lorries bearing a logo stating **SMD** and a very large and what seemed to be very thick shutter door through which the faint sounds of groaning could only just be deciphered. "Pot luck huh?" She said as she continued to scan the place noticing only one solitary door leading out of the room, which she knew would be the only way for them to go.

"Delivery Company or something I think." Frank said taking her hand and heading towards the door that she herself had been looking at. With his free hand he pressed down the handle and propped it open an inch before retrieving his pistol, he hoped it would be safe but doubted it somehow. The fact that they had found this place seemed impossible enough so he certainly wasn't expecting any more favours although they certainly fucking deserved a few considering what they had endured so far. As he peered into the new room there was simply a small corridor leading to four doors and a stairway, which at least meant that there were not many places for them to search or be attacked from.

"Let's search downstairs first." Abbey whispered from behind him knowing that the stumbling bastards couldn't climb very well up or down stairs, well she hoped not anyway as he nodded his agreement letting go of her grip as he approached the first room. Noticing that the door was ajar he leaned back and thrust his boot into the wood happy as it swung back and revealed a small toilet and sink within which although in need of a spring clean was certainly a welcomed sight. The second door received the same treatment and revealed a small office, the desk littered with invoices and other business paraphernalia but thankfully it was zombie free.

The third door had to be pushed open and as he entered the smell hit him immediately making his approach a lot more cautious. He turned to warn Abbey but the look of disgust on her face let him know that she had smelt it too and carried the same concern that he did. Again he took a step back and pushed the door as hard as he could with his boot aiming his gun immediately after as the door rushed open revealing the contents of the room within. Once again it seemed they were in luck as they both breathed a sigh of relief seeing the kitchen within. Rotten food lay on the table in its masses hinting that at some point someone or perhaps a small group had held up here although they had not exactly looked after the place, that was at least obvious.

Frank entered with Abbey behind him as he scanned the few cupboards and the small fridge a little disappointed that all they turned up were a few tins of food and drink but at least it was better than nothing. After a small search that turned up little more of any use they decided to search the upper floor, the final door downstairs being an exit to the outside which had been heavily bolted by whoever had been here before them which of course led them to wonder if this person were still within the confines of the building its self. The fact that it was bolted from the inside indicating to them that this could indeed be a possibility. As far as the door went, they had no need to touch this although a view of what lay outside would have been nice, so far all the windows were blacked out meaning that they were still clueless as to their whereabouts. Having travelled for three solid hours underground through water that varied in depth throughout their trek they could not realistically judge how far they had come so a view to the outside world to help them gather their bearings at least and would have been more than helpful for them.

Thankfully, as they continued their search the stairs brought no great drama either and all that awaited them at the summit was another short corridor but this time only two doors, one of which was already gaping wide open. It was simply a storage room holding only the most basic of cleaning products and judging on the state of the building and the layer of thick dust that covered the vacuum cleaner within the cupboard, cleanliness had not been a major part of this operation. Frank grabbed Abbey's hand once more rather than telling her to follow him to the final door. Should there be anything lurking inside he didn't want to alert the fuckers by being noisy as he made his approach suddenly feeling more nervous than he had so far, assuming simply that he felt this way as they were almost in the clear. He took his hand once more from Abbey's grip and placed it on the door, the gun also at the ready as he pushed as hard as he could, trying to go for the surprise option to anyone waiting within. The aroma of death hit them both instantly and they saw that the room ahead was indeed occupied although it certainly was not what they had expected. They both gasped aloud at what they saw shocked at the sight before them, the glassy eyes of the dead simply staring back at the intruders.

Chapter 14

Another hour of failed mayday attempts and her patience was growing seriously thin, as was the comfort of the chair on which she reluctantly sat. A broken spring constantly prodding her left buttock was enough to drive her round the bend especially as her attempts at finding any form of rescue had so far failed pretty miserably. She was still no closer to knowing if she was even using the radio correctly but then again she supposed she would never know unless someone finally answered her distress calls. Sure she was happy to be safe and secure with access to sufficient food and drink but the thought of being taken away from this fucking hellhole would always be at the very front of her mind which meant that she would keep up her radio attempts whether they were answered or not.

Even the simple thought of finding another survivor would do the job, so long as they didn't stab her in the back like her so called fucking friends had done on leaving the theatre. The thought of them made her temperature rise immediately as she felt the rage build furiously within herself. Those fucking bastards, she still couldn't believe that they had simply left her to die out there. She was so angry at the simple thought of the two treacherous fuckers that her hands began to tremble violently as tears began brimming at her eyes. It was with these intense emotions, that Shaznay momentarily ditched the radio attempts and decided to search the offices that she had at first attempt only glanced over. It was an activity that she hoped would uncover something useful but more so to stop the negative hate filled thoughts that were surging within her once more.

The fucking bastards. She doubted very much that the rooms would actually turn up anything but either way it was worth a try, besides she was ready for something to eat and the canteen was in the same direction as the offices that she planned to search. She just hoped that it did clear her mind, after all being stuck alone with her thoughts wasn't all that pleasant at the best of times especially when those thoughts became filled with anger and hatred.

After a small snack, it took her a few minutes of casually paced walking to reach the first of the rooms, a large plaque outside stating that it was or had been the commissioner's office which to her sounded very important although looking at the mess within it didn't really seem that it had been so whilst in use. The humongous oak desk could hardly be seen for the chaos on top, papers were strewn everywhere, the computer lay shattered on the ground along with a blood stained and tattered police uniform that by the looks of things had at least two bite marks on it. Shaznay didn't really need to guess that someone had probably either died or been fatally injured in this room at some point but she was at least glad that she had not been there to witness it or even to be on the receiving end of such an attack. She couldn't help but wonder momentarily if she had come across the previous occupant of the jacket and perhaps even filled their skull full of bullets but she soon shook of the macabre thoughts, a little surprised at herself for thinking them although with everything that she had witnessed it was hardly a shock that her mind should drift to a few dark areas.

She continued to glance around the room for a few moments more as she remained in the doorway hoping that something would catch her eye but nothing amongst the disarray seemed to jump immediately to her attention. There was a weapons locker toppled on its side that she had pondered but looking at the massive indentations around the lock someone had already failed in their attempts to gain entry so she was not about to waste any time or energy with the thick metal unit, she would rather reserve her strength for now should she need it for something more important.

Perhaps if she remained alone in the building for much longer she could always come back and tackle it but that was a consideration that she quickly pushed to the back of her mind as she approached what was easily the biggest desk she had ever seen. "He must have been important!" She said out loud to herself as she looked at the dusty name plaque that read 'Commissioner Neil Maltby' before talking another few steps to where three massive drawers were. She quickly opened all of them and found as she expected that if anything good had once lived in any of them it had long since been taken. As she sighed and brushed her hands through the mess of papers she found the phone, which she lifted to her ear with a smile on her face knowing in advance the silence that she would hear. With a large exhale she let herself fall backwards into the black leather swivel chair loving the comfort immediately on impact and watching as the black handset swung on its cord. No point putting the fucking thing back on the set she had thought feeling a little fed up with her lack of success so far since her entry to the police station. Sure she had found food and after the disposal of a few corpses she had found safety but in all reality she knew she was looking for more. Survivors or rescue, those were the things that she wanted and she knew it as she pushed off the desk with her leg in order to spin her seat in a circle.

She took a mental note to wheel the chair back to the communications room with her to replace the rickety old thing that she had been sitting on so far, this comfortable discovery a tiny bit of fortune she supposed although there were a million things she would have wished for over a relaxing seat given her current predicament. As she half-wittedly scanned the room for a third time, once again trying to find the willpower to search on despite the fact she assumed everything of value had most certainly disappeared a glisten in the corner of the room suddenly grabbed her attention tightly. Underneath a large empty wooden cupboard she could see a key, a little too big to fit some cuffs but perhaps big enough to fit the locker she had earlier examined. It was surely too good to be true but of course her instant curiosity took over as she stood quickly and began to move.

Her anticipation rose as she approached the large piece of furniture, crouched and retrieved the item before turning to her right and facing the metal locker thinking to herself that it could not possibly be the right key for the lock. She didn't bother to stand the item straight, as the access to the door was unhindered but out of sheer excitement she held her breath. At first she wondered if she did have the right key, her hope fading slightly as she tried to fit it in the lock unsuccessfully but her perseverance paid off as she continued with her attempts. The lock and surrounding metal had withstood a battering from whoever had tried to get in before her but after a couple of failed attempts and some simple brute force the key finally slid perfectly into place. She turned it rapidly and pulled the metal door open with all her might, the bent hinges squealing from the effort, as it swung open. As she peered inside she had expected to smile but the reaction didn't come, instead it was a look of complete shock that appeared on her stunned face. Shaznay was in complete awe of what she had just discovered, she couldn't believe it, her discovery was quite simply unbelievable.

She had eaten a tin of ravioli and taken a litre bottle of water back to the communications room with her along with her newest find which she had packed in a police backpack that had been retrieved from the armoury. It was this that she now unzipped and carefully emptied onto the ground between her legs, for what seemed like the hundredth time she simply shook her head wondering if and how they would come in handy and why the hell such things would have been kept in a police station. Christ before the zombies had arrived, street crime had been bad but she doubted somehow they would have ever dealt with it using these fucking things. At an army barracks she would have expected to find them for sure, but not here. The twelve grenades seemed to shine as she remained transfixed by them knowing that she had certainly stumbled on something very valuable to her survival, she had even thought that were she to become trapped she could at least die knowing she would take a large handful of the fuckers out too but hopefully it wouldn't come to that and she would be able to use them without the need to take her own life.

She continued to simply look at the explosives for quite some time more, the steady hiss of radio static in the background as she pondered her next action. She decided she would search the rest of the rooms in the hope of more precious finds before taking a trip to the roof to test one of the grenades. After all she had no idea how powerful they were, last thing she needed was to use one in a panic and blow her own bastard legs off and besides it would be a stress relief to obliterate some of those creatures which she admitted to herself was the main reason she wanted to set off one of the hand held explosives.

It had taken just under an hour to search the remaining rooms of which she had done an extremely thorough job, especially after she had managed to stumble on the key in the Commissioner's office. Unfortunately though there was nothing else for her to discover although she was hardly disappointed after the treasure that she already uncovered on her first search. In the first two rooms she had even gotten her hopes up as she had searched under the furniture before realising she was kidding herself thinking that fortune would strike twice but overall she was certainly ecstatic with the result she had been given.

It was now as she walked towards the roof exit that the smile began to grow on her face as she held the solitary grenade tightly in her moist left palm. She had never really had the luxury to enjoy killing any of these things as her life had always been in a certain amount of danger but now it was different, it was time for her to take a little much needed revenge. She was past the whole tragedy, grief and pain of the whole situation now and beginning to accept the fact that she was surrounded by the end of the world and it was with this in mind that she would have a little fun. She was in complete control of this situation and despite the fact she knew it was kind of sadistic, she would enjoy every last moment of what she was about to do, the bastards could pay for the pain that they had caused her throughout this whole nightmare. The cold air and rain blasted her face as she walked through the fire door to reach the roof, which seemed it had once been used as a smoker's hangout when the station had still been functional.

She had not noticed the vast amount of discarded cigarette butts on her first trip out there but then again it had only been a quick scout for any remaining zombies of which there had thankfully been none. It was now for the first time in God knows how long that she craved a cigarette realising that she had managed to quit without so much as thinking about it. Not through choice of course but the situation had simply forced it upon her. It was with this thought still in mind that she walked over to the edge of the roof, peering down at the street below glad for once to see there were plenty of undead skulking around on the pavement. She reached back and grabbed her pistol, taking aim and firing one shot directly below her square into the skull of one of the monsters. The creature that had once been an elderly woman dropped to the pavement immediately and lay still for quite some time before dragging her rotting body slowly back to a standing position. Shaznay watched on amused but at the same time hating that fact that the fuckers were so hard to kill, if only it were like in the movies where a headshot did the trick life would certainly be that little bit easier. Unfortunately though she knew only too well that it was not so as she looked once more at the grenade that she still held.

One more look down below was all it took for her to pull the pin and toss the explosive downwards although far enough away as not to blow through the wall of the station, or so she hoped. As she heard the metal clink on the concrete below, she crouched somewhat wanting to see the result as the five seconds she had to wait ticked agonisingly by. There were six of the creatures in the direct vicinity of the grenade when it detonated and each one of them seemed to go up in a cloud of red mist as the giant boom erupted into the air echoing down the surrounding streets. Shaznay jumped at the noise and took in the short-lived spectacle and the unbelievable aftermath that she had to blink rapidly at just to believe. She had assumed that the explosives would be good but not as destructive as what had just happened in front of her very eyes. All of the zombies within a twenty foot radius had been affected in some way by the blast and quite badly too. Most of them had either been decapitated or suffered some form of limb amputation, which told her immediately that she had discovered frag grenades rather than what she had first thought were the standard type.

The fact that she hadn't blown through the station windows was more than a surprise too after what had just occurred but she was certainly more than impressed with the power that they contained. The thought bizarrely crossed her mind that had she not owned an X Box and a few war games then she would have no way of guessing the types of weaponry she held but her focus soon drifted back to the carnage below which she still watched in awe and amazement as the few surviving zombies tried to move with their various newly sustained injuries.

Twenty minutes of observation passed before Shaznay finally left the rooftop and returned back to the communications room, this time with the comfortable chair from the commissioner's office and a half pack of smokes that she had found up above. It was once again time to radio for help although her hopes of gaining an answer still remained at an all time low. At least she had her grenades and her cigarettes though which for now certainly would keep a smile on her face.

Chapter 15

He sat at the table, a bundle of paper clutched in his bony fingers and his mouth open in a silent never-ending scream. From the sight and smell it was not difficult to tell that he had been dead for quite some time, decay already taking a hold of the once pink flesh. A gun was gripped tightly in his other hand and going by the gaping hole in his forehead it was not difficult to see that whoever he was, suicide had been his personal form of escape from the surrounding hell.

After a few moments of simply staring at the motionless figure Abbey pointed for Frank to look at the corpse's arm, which he immediately did, noticing the bite mark that she had meant and therefore understanding a little more behind the man's unfortunate demise. It seemed that there was a motive behind the man's self inflicted death than just cowardice or panic and they certainly couldn't blame him for that after seeing what had quite obviously happened to him. They had both previously stated that they would rather die than to become a mindless wandering corpse and in their now deceased friend Sean they had seen such a promise become a truth at first hand as he had taken his life thanks to a bite from one of those bastard things.

Abbey cautiously approached the body, wondering momentarily what this man had lost in life through this hell before he had taken the chance to extinguish his own light. She stopped a couple of feet away from him, noticing sadly that he had not been all that old perhaps twenty three at the most although she knew very well that millions younger than him had also died so far but still she couldn't help this feeling that had crept up thanks to the sight in front of her. She exhaled sorrowfully as she reached forward and took the paper which tore slightly as she pulled it from his tightly rigour mortised grasp. She looked up at Frank as she unrolled the paper; he gave her a slight smile for reassurance more than anything else as she began to read the letter out loud.

"Should anyone ever find this note then let me congratulate you on being a lucky son of a bitch, how you survived this much shit hitting the fan I have no idea but give yourself a pat on the back and a shiny gold medal. Hell, give yourself two medals and a brass fucking band. My name is Paul Barnet and as you will be able to see I did not fare so well although I did last as long as I humanly could which was certainly more than a lot of the population could. There were five of us here at the firm on the day that it came, spreading like a plague it was on top of us and the city centre before we could even fucking blink, for slow thick fuckers those zombie's move bloody fast in numbers. Everything just happened so fucking rapidly we couldn't react, it was suddenly hell on earth and there was nothing that anyone could do about it. We had no real weapons apart from my pistol and the tools we keep here but what good is a fucking crowbar and a handgun against an army of the dead? On the same note I soon found out how little my gun actually did being as though you need to behead the fuckers to stop them, which left us with pretty much no defence against the masses of corpses outside. Two of the mechanics stupidly tried to make a dash for it in one of the cars, after all it is only a ten-minute drive to get to Nottingham but they didn't even make the end of the street. It was just mayhem, another car hit them head on and boom, the petrol tank went up like a fucking firework, they had no chance at all in that inferno but I suppose thinking about it rather that way out than being eaten. Everyone everywhere was just in a mass panic from the word go and there was so much screaming, it was unbearable both to watch and listen to. Seeing all those people torn to shreds and eaten alive we had to simply barricade ourselves in, we had no other choice unless we wanted to end up the same bloody way as everyone else. Escape just wasn't possible. If those evil things didn't kill you, some crazy bastard trying to escape would have either run you over or used you as a human shield in their own attempts to survive.

It was after this that the waiting began, the rescue of course never came and the sightings of other survivors diminished into zero leaving the three of us that remained feeling more and more alone knowing that *the few rations that we had were running lower and lower with each fucked up day that ticked by. Luckily we knew we were pretty safe in here but that wasn't enough as the time for us to make a run for it had come despite the fact we knew it would probably spell the end. We knew the city would be teeming with the bastards but it was the only way that we knew might even have a chance of working and the only place we knew we could find some form of weaponry or help. As I am sure you have guessed our attempted escape failed miserably which led me of course to my current deceased state. We couldn't take the trucks due to all the abandoned cars everywhere, so we decided armed with one pistol, our crowbars and our wrenches that we would simply beat our way through the army, it was a poor plan but it was all we had apart from starvation. We lasted all of about three minutes! Kieran Gannon the admin guy had his throat ripped out first and Jim Stones, one of the drivers died trying his hardest to save him from the attacking corpses. I should have just kept on running but seeing two guys who you work with every day of the damn week getting eaten kind of stops you in your tracks which was when the bastard fucking bit me. I screamed and emptied three rounds into its skull before retreating back to the compound knowing instantly that I was fucked, I could have stayed out there and died but there is no way I was risking coming back as one of them mindless bastards which is why I came up here instead.*

Despite the fact that I am about to put a bullet through my head I just tried to radio for help one last time but I have had the same result as all the attempts I have tried which is complete silence. It has been like that for a long time now, which does not bode well for the rest of the country. I fear I could even be the last one alive but not for long now. I only wrote this to prolong my suicide but I feel very unwell now and I can only assume it is the bite beginning to change me, my blood almost itches and I feel hungry and sick at the same time. A cold sweat has drenched my clothing and the sight of the blood dripping from my wound almost turns me on. I don't want to be one of them and at the same time I don't want to end my own life but I know I am rapidly turning into a fucking cannibal. I have even tried to eat and drink some of the few morsels of food left here in the building but still I feel thirsty and hungry, it is the most bizarre feeling and certainly not a pleasant one to have. I think I had better go now. If anyone does find this, kill the bastards for my work crew and for me. Kill each and every one of the rotten, stumbling, worm ridden motherfuckers. Oh and should you find my body walking around like those cunts outside, I beg you to cut off my fucking head."

    She placed the letter on the table in front of his stiff cold body, her feeling of sadness now even more present knowing that he had been through such an ordeal himself, having to face being bitten and the consequences there after must have been indescribable for him. At least with Sean he had taken the instant decision to literally bite the bullet but not this poor bastard, it had been obvious that he had wanted so badly to survive he had delayed his inevitable end as much as he could. She soon felt Franks arm on her shoulder, his reassuring touch helping her somewhat as she looked at him and smiled through the sadness that she was feeling. For the first time in the short while she had known this man she realised just how much of a calming affect he had on her although as she studied his features briefly she couldn't pinpoint exactly what it was about him that did the trick.

    Despite the rugged overgrown stubble, the hair that was well overdue a cut and his dirty clothes he was quite handsome and seemed to have the personality to match his rugged looks. From the brief moments he had spoken about his deceased partner it was obvious that he was a deeply caring young man and that certainly matched her own passionate and loving nature. It wasn't that she was looking for anything romantic with him although she would have been lying to herself if she had said that she wasn't attracted to this man. These thoughts certainly took her by surprise being as they had both recently lost their loved ones in this whole mess. She could only suppose that it was the shit situation that they were in that seemed to be bringing her closer to him but at the end of the day she knew that she couldn't help any of what was happening even if she wanted to. Still though the fact that he made her feel safe and calm was what she needed right now to keep her going especially being as it was just the two of them, everything else like the connection that she had begun to feel she would just have to take as it came. Life was now more than ever too fucking short to worry about the small things.

After a few moments longer, Frank finally released his touch on her. "Let's try and get the fuck out of here." He said motioning towards the large grey radio system behind both Abbey and the deceased Paul Barnet knowing that a change of tone was needed after their discovery of the body. With a smile she stepped past the dead man and walked straight over to the machine. "Let's hope someone's listening," she replied before taking the microphone and pressing the large power button in front of her.

Frank had noticed the way she had looked at him earlier and also the way she had responded to him touching her shoulder. Strangely he also felt something despite the continuing rage that burned within him thanks to the loss that he had suffered. He missed Sharon so much it crushed him and he knew that no matter what he would never ever stop loving her, she had been so amazing but that still didn't stop what he was feeling now towards this new woman in his life. Sure he felt guilt and pain but he accepted the fact that as a human he was powerless to fight his emotions, after all it was something out of his control. He felt drawn to her and even though he was the man in this situation, he felt safe with her and on top of this she was a very beautiful woman. He knew that it was their loneliness and the fact that they shared very similar losses that was pushing them towards each other in the way that it was but there was little point in him fighting it, not now. He wasn't about to go and try his luck with her though, he wasn't ready for anything like that but for things to unfold at their own pace was fine by him. After all he knew that they only had each other and to get through this they would need every bit of strength and positive motivation that they could get.

A few unanswered help calls had been spoken by Abbey but only the static responded to her words confirming their thoughts that most likely no one was listening, not on the frequency that they were trying at least. Frank located a large dial, which he began to steadily turn, the alterations in the various crackles telling him that he must be doing something right in his search to find at least some form of outside communication. The two of them both had doubts that they would discover anyone else alive but they would never lose hope in their search both for survival and possibly rescue. To do so would admit defeat and they would simply have to accept that this constant effort just to exist was their only future, which didn't really fill them with any form of excitement or optimism. They just had to cling to the hope that something was out there somewhere, not only that, they would find that something too.

As Frank continued his so far fruitless efforts he glanced across at his companion who was in turn looking back directly at him. Abbey smiled although never removed her gaze from his as they locked eyes and the tension between them suddenly increased massively. In a situation where normally one person would be forced to look away, neither of them did as their locked gaze continued uninterrupted. Abbey knew she had been caught almost leering at him and there was little chance in hiding it by quickly now simply by looking away. 'Busted!' Were her thoughts at first but as he now smiled back she knew there was nothing for her to be embarrassed about. He was feeling the same things that she was and now she was sure of it as she placed the mouthpiece back on the console and slowly walked the five paces that were between the two of them. Frank stopped his movements on the machine and stood straight facing her as she walked up to him, her face so close to his own as she looked up so that he could feel her warm breath on his neck. As they stared deeply into each other's eyes, neither spoke a word, they were both too locked into each other as their temperatures rose and their hearts increased in pace.

It seemed like an eternity ticked by before they almost lunged at each other, their kiss so passionate and frenzied that they soon had to part for breath, gasping from the intensity of their passion. Once again their eyes met, Frank begun smiling as Abbey bit her lower lip and started to slowly remove his t-shirt. She admired his athletically toned body as she slipped out of the buttoned blouse that she wore revealing her pert naked breasts. Frank grabbed her once again as their lips met for a second time even more passionately as they enjoyed the taste of each other, their bodies slowly sliding down to the floor beneath them. They continued kissing for an age, just enjoying the closeness but all the while wanting and needing each other more as they slowly and tenderly undressed each other until they were both naked side by side. Abbey gently pushed him onto his back and sat upon him, gasping with pleasure as he entered her. She began moving slowly at first before gradually increasing her gyrating hips. As he kissed her neck softly he felt her beginning to tense, her gently moans growing louder as he felt his own pleasure building within. She lifted her head and kissed him heavily before biting into his lower lip as the surges of her orgasm began, as she began to shake she felt Frank reach his climax too as she collapsed on top of him exhausted from the pleasure that surged through her so strongly. Their sweaty bodies were like one as he held her tightly to him, running his fingers through her hair and kissing her sweat-covered brow. They remained in their passionate embrace, unwilling to move, both breathing heavily and feeling relaxed and safer than they had felt in a very long time.

"I'm so glad you're here with me." Abbey spoke softly as she kissed his cheek feeling a warmth inside as his hug tightened and he gently brushed his hand through her hair once again.

"I'll be back in a minute." Frank suddenly spoke as he gently rolled her to one side and began to rise to his feet. She looked up a little shocked and ready to ask where he was going but before she got chance his glistening naked body had left the room leaving her momentarily alone. She waited a little anxiously wondering what she had done wrong but as he returned with a blanket, some food and drink her beaming smile soon replacing the look of worry she had momentarily worn.

Frank looked appraisingly over her stunning body before laying down and draping the cover over both of them holding her immediately once more in his embrace. They ate and drank, both unable to stop the amazing feelings that surged within them before they once again sank into a deep clinch. They somehow found the energy to enjoy each other's bodies once again before the stress and sleep deprivation finally took its toll, both of them drifting into unconsciousness in each other's loving grasp with the faint sounds of static filling the room.

Chapter 16

"Holy shit!" Were the words that escaped her lips, she had heard someone she was sure of it, it couldn't have been a dream. Abbey scrambled to a seated position shaking Frank rapidly to wake him from his slumber still struggling to comprehend what she knew that she had heard. His eyes snapped open immediately; concern gripped him at first as he hazily stared around the room thankful when Abbey told him all was well and that there was no need for him to panic. "There was someone on the radio I swear." She spoke loudly and animatedly as she slipped into her knickers and her blouse as quickly as she possibly could. Frank rose too albeit a little slower due to the clinging sleep that he still felt, dressing only in his boxers as he followed her over to the console where she hastily grabbed the mouthpiece in her left hand that he noticed was shaking through anticipation. As she pushed in the button and asked if anyone was there the following seconds of waiting passed slower than she had ever known time go by. God she hoped she was right and that it hadn't been a dream.

Shaznay had been repeatedly attempting contact for longer than she dared guess and once again she was growing tired of her failed efforts, she had said mayday so many times now the word sounded almost alien to her. Any hopes that had remained within were rapidly fading, deep down she knew how fucked up everything was outside and the fact that she had survived never mind anyone else was quite miraculous. Perhaps she was actually the last one, she just fucking hoped not as it was the most depressing thought she could imagine. Still though she knew she might as well continue with her apparently wasted efforts at finding rescue, there was little else for her to do in the station apart from eating, sleeping and shooting zombies from the roof top or the upper floor windows which she had decided would be her next task to pass some time and keep her mind occupied. Anything to stop the probable pending insanity from taking a hold, after all she knew that a life of solitude would eventually bring out the crazy in her. At least for now she remained sane though as she decided to carry on with the radio for a few minutes longer although she saw little reason why she should bother. Bursting some skulls with the few weapons she carried was much more satisfying than these one way radio conversations that so far had served no purpose apart from lowering her mood and making her believe she was the sole survivor of this apocalypse.

As she called out with mayday once more the static suddenly hissed violently making her jump backwards and almost topple over in her commissioner's chair. It was as she looked wide eyed at the various little displays in front of her that she heard the voice. The static crackle stopped and there it was, as clear as day and she just couldn't believe it, someone else was fucking alive as she rapidly began speaking herself desperate to make contact with whoever this woman was. "Hello, hello. Are you there? My names Shaznay and I am at the police station in Nottingham, over."

The wait for a response was agonising but as she heard the reply to her statement tears began streaming down her face immediately, she was unable to control her instant joy and emotion at the sounds she had almost given up on hearing. This person could possibly be on the opposite side of the world to her but that thought never entered her mind, just knowing that someone else had made it through this hell made them seem as though they were right next to her holding her hand through this fucked up mess. It felt like a miracle, having begun to give up all hope it seemed that finally her perseverance and determination seemed to be paying off.

"Oh, my God. I can't believe there is someone else. How many of you are there and are you somewhere safe? Is there rescue?" Was the excitable reply, which to Shaznay sounded like it came from a woman that couldn't have been much older or younger than herself. She explained that she was alone and that her efforts for gaining rescue had so far been a waste of time but that she was now thankfully well armed and pretty damn safe too considering there were zombies everywhere. "Where are you and are you alone?" She asked hoping and praying that it was a larger group but either way knowing she could count herself lucky just to have found one person amongst the ongoing nightmare plague. Even if they did turn out to be million miles away at least it was human contact, she had begun to wonder how long she would have continued wilfully surviving alone with no one for company but herself and the army of carcasses outside.

"Two of us here but not sure where we are, could be anywhere from Sheffield to right on your doorstep, we have been travelling in the sewers so we have no idea of how much ground we have covered but if you hang on ten minutes we will try find out so please whatever you do, don't change the frequency."

With that the line suddenly went back to the usual hiss of static and radio silence was once again quickly resumed although for once Shaznay really didn't care, the crackling noise sounded heavenly now that she knew she wasn't alone anymore. She sat back in her comfortable chair and rubbed her eyes exhaling at the same time as she felt a massive load lift from her tense shoulders. Her hope was suddenly at its highest since this nightmare had begun and once more she had something to fight for since the day her friends had deserted her which now because of this piece of luck seemed like a lifetime ago. She knew that she could always try and get back to the theatre in an attempt to rescue her friends but she wasn't that stupid and besides they didn't deserve her fucking help or anyone else's for that matter.

Were she to even attempt it, chances are she would die trying and besides the only one of the group worth saving would more than likely be dead already. The thought of this did sadden her as it entered her mind but she quickly dismissed the image of how ashen faced her dying friend had been. At the end of the day she knew there was little she could have done end of story. That was why she had remained at the station rather than trying to save him, she would only help herself now and besides she had safety, food and water along with a radio, which seemed now had proven more useful than she had begun to think it ever could. She could only hope that her one true friend had died peacefully and pain free in the end and that the other two fuckers had been eaten alive for what they had done to her. They actually deserved the one fate that was worse than death.

Shaznay soon pushed the thoughts of her previous refuge to the back of her mind as she placed her feet on the console and lay back comfortably in her seat. She lit a cigarette and exhaled the smoke towards the ceiling, a beaming smile etched on her features as she basked in her newfound joy. She simply couldn't believe her luck.

Abbey hugged Frank tightly squeezing as hard as she possibly could, they couldn't believe that they had found someone, and so bloody quickly at that. They knew of course that they had been unbelievably fortunate Shaznay informing them that she had been trying to contact someone for days without success. This mattered little though as they accepted the fact they had found a very small needle in a very large haystack. On discovering her they had increased their hopes and their will to fight on further through the terror and they could not be more grateful for their fortune. The only slight setback they now faced was of course getting to her and also finding out where the hell they were in the first place. They prayed it was quite close to Nottingham city centre but realistically they had no way of guessing their location for sure. They knew they had to be within a decent vicinity though, just the logic from where they had started out and the rough direction they had been heading told them that much but with the streets in the condition they were, close didn't mean that it would be safe or even quick to try and reach this new destination.

"Come on then, let's see if we can figure out where the fuck this place is." Were Frank's words as he released the embrace and smiled at her before giving her a long kiss on the mouth. Abbey grinned back at him as he winked before turning to the few papers that were spread on the table, some of which he noted thankfully were invoices that had seemingly never made it as far as the little office downstairs. It only took a few moments of matching the depot address, which was for a Same Day Packages, or SMD, which to his joy and disbelief was stated as being in Nottingham to the logo that they had seen downstairs on the trucks. Looking at the postcode numbers their location was more than likely the outskirts of the city but still at least they were close enough to the police station that they could possibly make it there within a reasonable amount of time. The fact that they happened to be within any form of close distance of this person was a fucking phenomenon and he knew it.

As he happily told Abbey how close they were neither of them could believe how far they had travelled but not only that it had proven to be in a very helpful direction. They knew though that despite this they faced the challenge of reaching the woman on the other end of the radio, which would more, than likely throw them head first into God only knew how many deadly situations. Once again though, it was simply a task that they had to take on.

As Abbey took the mouthpiece once more and began explaining their findings to Shaznay, Frank decided to go on a little hunt, were they to have any hope of finding her then they would need a map of some kind to help them. After all they knew that the safest and probably only way for them to travel would be once again in the shit filled sewers in which case they would once again be travelling quite blindly but at least safely. Any directional help they could get would be needed, he just hoped that the sewers would correspond with the streets above or at least keep them close to a path or direction they could follow but he supposed they would just have to find out the hard way.

Shaznay sat back and breathed a sigh of relief after ending her second conversation with Abbey. She had been informed that the couple had located a map and once they were told the street name of the station they had found where she was almost immediately. It seemed that they were about four or five miles away, which once again had left both parties shocked at their luck and fortune. The fact that they were possibly the only remaining survivors and just happened to be so close to one another was pretty astounding to say the least.

She didn't envy them one bit though, having to travel through the sewers and possibly amongst the dead at street level was as dangerous as it got but she knew it was the only plan that made sense. It had been fucking hard for her on leaving the theatre to survive amongst the dead and these two had to now make it a lot further than she had done. As things currently were she was certainly better off than they were, after all she was in a secure police station with plenty of food, water and weaponry whereas from the little she had heard they were in a delivery warehouse of some kind and now had to go waltzing around a fucking army of the damned. She could only hope that they would make it to her in one piece but for now there was little that she could do apart from cross her fingers and toes and simply wait. They had confirmed to her that they would set off immediately and she would just wait and watch out for their arrival, which she knew could take any amount of time depending on any difficulties that they may come across during their journey. Worst of all if they were to die she would have no way of knowing, resulting of course in a permanent state of expectancy. That mattered little to her though, the excitement of finding other survivors and not being alone for the rest of eternity would be enough to keep her waiting for hours, days and even weeks on end that was for sure.

As she stood and stretched she had only one plan in mind, she would grab a blanket, some food and drink and head up to the rooftop although there was no mad rush. Logic told her that the fastest they would reach her would probably be two hours so she could at least take her time gathering what she needed for her wait. She had told the two of them to try and approach the building from the front, which she knew would be the easiest way to see them and let them in. In the meantime she would begin clearing the way, she knew there were masses of the fuckers on the main road but that mattered little, she had enough ammo to deal with the bastards and it would at least be an entertaining wait for them to arrive. She would pick each and every one of them off, one by one.

Chapter 17

The smell was as usual horrendous but thankfully the going had been quite easy so far considering they were wading thigh deep in faeces. They were pretty certain from the minimal amount of kinks in the tunnel they were still following the road that would lead them most of the way to their goal. They at least hoped so anyway. It had been a few hours now since they had left the safety of the delivery unit but it had been for the best despite the feeling of danger they both felt now they were travelling beneath the zombie's once again. The deaths of Matt, Rhianne and Sean still hung vividly in their minds but thankfully they still had each other and the passion that they had now discovered to keep them fighting on. It was definitely what they had needed and it seemed it was for now more than enough to keep them going in order to find their destination.

About forty minutes into their trek, Abbey had stopped Frank pulled him to her before kissing him hard and passionately without even saying a word. She had begun walking again immediately afterwards glancing at him only once with a cheeky smile that he could just about make out in the torchlight.

"What was that for?" He had asked, his voice unable to hide the pleasure he had felt at what had just occurred.

"Do I need a reason?" She had responded simply before taking his hand and increasing her pace despite the thick goop that they trudged through. "Let's check the street up there." She had said as she had led him to a rusted metal ladder. They had known that the distance to the station hadn't been covered but occasional checks to the surface let them know what the hell was happening up there and helped with the claustrophobia that the sewer tunnels caused. There was of course always the chance that they would recognise something too but so far they had come across nothing of familiarity, the fact that neither of them were massively familiar with the city not really helping things.

As they carried on their hike, Frank allowed himself another smile thinking about the kiss that he had received wondering momentarily if he was falling for her more than he had first thought. It didn't take long for him to confirm to himself that he was, in a big way too which he couldn't deny. He was surprised but then again he couldn't blame himself and neither could she for these emotions that had swept over them so suddenly. This crisis had brought them together and the way things had gone for them since the shit hit the fan in the first place they deserved what they had found in each other and he intended to cherish every moment that they had together.

He knew and accepted that this passion that they had found could quite easily be taken away from them in the blink of an eye. He glanced across at her and noticed she was busy paying attention to her footing on the slippery floor as he squeezed her hand making her turn unsteadily towards him, almost losing her balance in the process. With a slight laugh Frank repaid her earlier kiss with the same action, slowly at first but more passionately as she responded, her hand reaching up inside his shirt and feeling his muscled chest beneath. Their embrace lasted for over a minute, the heat and enthusiasm between them growing rapidly, both feeling the urge for each other's bodies once more as they finally parted, both gasping for breath. As Frank looked deep into her eyes feeling the warmth from her body he tilted his head towards the ladders next to where she stood. "Your turn sweetie." He spoke softly feeling her nudge him sarcastically before she turned and begun clambering to the top. So far any grates that had needed shifting, he had taken care of however the gaps that lined some of the pavements had been Abbey's to deal with. As she reached the top and begun to peer through, craning her neck in an attempt to see outside she felt a pinch on her backside as she kicked out slightly grinning from ear to ear as she did so, looking quickly down and calling him a cheeky bastard in the process.

It was as she tried to refocus that she noticed something that she was sure she recognised, she had to blink twice but it was definitely there in front of her very eyes. The Victoria shopping centre was as bright as day and although her knowledge of the city was pretty vague she certainly knew this place and she knew that it was very close to where they needed to be. It was practically on the fucking doorstep.

His head erupted with a shower of crimson and seconds later his dead lifeless body hit the concrete with a dull thud. Shaznay reloaded the sniper rifle for the umpteenth time before placing it on the floor and retrieving her handgun wanting a bit more of a challenge with the last few visible zombies. There had been at a guess close to fifty of the fuckers at first however now only the smallest handful remained visible to her. She had taken her time with them, possibly taking them out in a slightly sadistic fashion but what the fuck did that matter she had supposed as she had blown out a few kneecaps and also taken a few groin shots before popping the skulls of those monsters that had been floored. After all the bastard things couldn't exactly feel pain and she had some time to burn which was exactly what she had been doing until now. It hadn't helped that the fuckers had to be beheaded in order to stop them which took an age when using the weapons she had. The easiest option available to her had simply been to disable the fuckers rather than to decapitate them all.

She assumed that about two and a half to three hours had crawled by since she had been on the rooftop and with no way of knowing how much longer she would be waiting she couldn't help but wish she had brought a little more food along for her stake out. The few morsels she had brought with her had found their home in the pit of her stomach along with most of the juice that she had.

Not only that she was running low on smokes too although she was unsure where she would find more within the station once she had smoked her last one. She knew at present though there was little she could really do about this problem as she lifted her pistol and took aim at a rotting woman at the opposite side of the street. Hungry, thirsty or craving there was no way in hell she would risk leaving her watch post even for the shortest time, she wanted to be ready when the two of them arrived, after all she had to sprint downstairs and unlock the door for them meaning that any hesitation could be deadly. The last thing she wanted was for them to turn up and be stuck outside amongst the dead while she busied herself with a tin of soup, or a search for some Benson and Hedges. Her food could wait. It probably wouldn't be that welcoming a sight if they were to arrive to a bolted door either, they would have surely been through enough shit on their journey to find her.

Shaznay held her breath for extra stability as she finally squeezed the trigger, the bang echoing around the street as a chunk of the woman's neck was obliterated leaving her head to hang awkwardly to the left. The injury inflicted seemed to bother the corpse little though as her shuffling continued, a gargle coming from her mouth to add to the chorus of groans that hung constantly on the air in every direction. Shaznay shook her head before pulling the trigger twice more.

The resilience of these things still amazed her, despite the fact they were dead she just couldn't seem to get her head round the difficulty it took to stop the bastards completely. The second and third bullets, like the first also hit home leaving nothing left of the creatures face except a reddish grey mush, which seemed to finally do the trick as her body became limp and hit the deck, the remains of her head coming free from the jolt of her falling impact. With a sigh, Shaznay lowered the weapon and rubbed her eyes, the constant targeting had taken its toll somewhat as she yawned but happily noticed just how many of the things she had so far immobilised. After all beheading or immobilising forty or so people with nothing but a rifle and a hand gun wasn't the easiest task as she had found out the hard way although she had at least found it quite a good and satisfying way to pass the time.

Not only that she had discovered that she was frighteningly accurate with both a rifle and much more impressively a pistol. Had there been any active police officers to see her shooting, she couldn't help but think they would have had her on the armed unit in a heartbeat. Whilst on the roof, she had quite easily been tempted to start tossing grenades at the zombies below but she knew it would have been quite wasteful although it would certainly have been a fun way to dispose of the monsters. She had instead though opted for her other weapons which now through patience and hard work had pretty much cleared the entire street of the walking dead.

As Shaznay began scanning the sights before her, thanks to her sharp shooting she saw the heaps of grounded or motionless bodies scattered all around. On the pavements and road there was now little danger apart from the six creatures that remained upright. She had certainly cleared the way for Abbey and Frank once they arrived but unfortunately she had no way of telling when that would be. She had accepted that days could pass depending on any troubles that they may face but a hope within told her they would arrive at any moment. For now though, all she could do was ensure she kept the front of the building monster free and that was what she intended on doing as she once again took aim at the closest zombie to her. The crack of gunfire erupted another four times into the air as dawn slowly began to emerge. Yet another demon hit the concrete and her weapon was once more reloaded with a fresh mag. God she hoped they made it to her safely.

Chapter 18

They had made it to street level after a long final embrace together, both accepting that they had now reached the dangerous and quite possibly deadly part of their trip. Despite the disgusting and claustrophobic nature of their journey so far it had probably been a walk in the park compared to what they would still face on the surface. The streets were simply teeming with the fuckers and both Abbey and Frank had accepted that they could very well die at any point regardless of how far they had made it and their will to survive. Armed only with their hand guns and a few close range weapons they were going to have to rely on their speed and agility to make it the half mile or so to the police station where their safety lay in waiting. It was a now or never moment and the apprehension that they felt was overwhelming.

"I am really glad I found you, and I hope you know that I would have fallen for you regardless of this situation." Abbey had spoken softly to him as a tear had run down her face only moments before they had surfaced from the sewers below and he had known and felt the authenticity in her comment despite their brief time together as lovers. He had smiled at her and replied with a simple 'me too' before kissing her softly, taking her hand and leading her cautiously to the surface trying to control the fact that he was shaking through fear and anticipation. It seemed that their feelings were growing closer at a fast speed with neither of them wanting this surprise joy that they had found to end, it had given them an extra reason to carry on past every obstacle that they faced and it had given them the belief and strength that they would need for this pending sprint to the finish line.

They had double and triple checked the map pretty much memorizing the way that they needed to go knowing very well that any wasted second or any slight indecisiveness would most probably result in their death. Luckily on surfacing they were fortunate enough to have a ten-metre breathing space as they looked around noticing for the first time that the gigantic shopping centre that they faced stood almost in complete ruins. Only a few windows remained unbroken and there were bodies and inedible remains scattered everywhere. It wasn't hard to tell that those poor bastards that now lay strewn across the streets had seemingly tried to take refuge within the gargantuan building. Their attempts had obviously failed. It was a sickeningly sad sight but not one that they could dwell on as he felt Abbey tug his hand as she set off towards the station in a swift jog, not wanting to linger in the same place for any longer than they already had.

They were more than glad that the sun was rising, the light enabling great visibility of any attacks that could come their way, which they hoped, would be in their minimum. Both had their weapons drawn ready and it was Abbey who took the first shot, the recoil of her weapon making her palm throb as she saw the bullet hit its intended target pretty much where she had aimed. The jaw of the closest zombie seemed to explode from the impact as a shower of red sprayed skywards and the monster collapsed in a heap clearing more space for the two of them to run. Despite the fact that the head shot wasn't enough to terminate them it certainly left them grounded long enough for them to pass safely without the risk of a bite as Frank let off two shots himself, the first of which missed the mark, the second however finding its way home. Shooting whilst on the run was certainly no easy task but unfortunately for them they simply didn't have the time to stop and take a proper aim at the rotting targets in their way.

Running down the side of the shopping mall rather than through it, the going was hard but manageable which was all they could really ask for considering the state of everything that they could see. Trying to conserve ammo they were dodging the majority of surrounding zombies as they approached a junction ahead where they knew a left turn would take them straight to their destination. As they quickly crossed the road, Frank placing a kick to one of the monsters throats to ensure a safe crossing a crack of gunfire erupted although this time to their utter joy it wasn't from either of them. Abbey looked quickly at Frank as he smiled at her happily through his heavy breathing, knowing that they were almost there. They had fucking made it.

She couldn't help but grin slightly at what had just occurred. The force of the bullet had sent the zombie backwards through a shop window where it now lay impaled on a large shard of glass wriggling away trying to get free. It was not quite the result she had wanted but it certainly worked and it had provided her with a moments worth of personal amusement so she wasn't about to complain at her unusually off centre shot.

Shaznay had heard the other sounds of gunfire in the distance growing closer with each one that rang out around the city centre, which meant thankfully that the two survivors had almost made it to her. Either that or there were more people that just happened to be near her which she doubted very much. Either way though she was ready, the way had now been cleared completely as she watched eagerly for Frank and Abbey's arrival, the door keys in her hand as she prepared to sprint downstairs and unlock the front door for them. Occasionally another zombie would creep into view which would then be quickly dealt with, caution taken of course that she didn't accidentally open fire on her two expected guests that could burst onto the scene at any point. She was making sure that the two members of the living population had a free and easy run to the entrance, there would be no last minute slip ups of that she was certain as she used all her will to simply concentrate on the street below. The anticipation that she felt was now immense, the thought that she was not alone and that she soon would have human company once again evoked an excitement within her that she struggled to contain.

The big smile now a permanent fixture on her face as she waited impatiently for them to arrive. As she brushed a strand of hair from her lip they finally burst into view from the left hand side of her vision. "Over here!" Were the two words she screamed immediately as she discarded her rifle to the floor and begun jumping and waving to get their attention. The action worked immediately as they both began grinning insanely and began pointing towards the two double doors below where Shaznay stood. She gave them the thumbs up and turned to begin her quick journey downstairs knowing that thanks to her many gunshots there would be no risk of any attacks. Despite this, she took the steps three at a time almost stumbling in her excitement beaming with joy when she reached the glass and saw the two figures breathing heavily waiting at the other side for her. With a quick turn of the key in all three locks the job was quickly done as they almost fell safely inside, Shaznay bolting the door quickly behind them once again. She had known that there was little need for such a rush, she had after all seen to it that there were no zombies within quite some distance of the front door but as always the better safe than sorry method would never be a bad thing to use.

   The trio hugged immediately despite the fact that they had never met before, it seemed natural for them to greet this way after all they had been through simply to last this long it gave them a sense of connection. The fact that they were probably the only survivors was more than enough to make them feel so close, remaining in their embrace that carried on for quite some time. As they eventually broke their grip on one another Shaznay immediately took them through to the canteen without really speaking first. She knew that from their travels they would be tired and probably hungry so she would not bombard them with questions just yet until she had at least let them rest for a minute, although she was sure they would want to know just as much information from her as she did from them. There would be a lot to talk about of that she was sure.

   As midday crawled by the group remained in the canteen, each with the remnants of both breakfast and dinner on the table in front of them. Despite the tiredness of all three of them they continued locked in conversation, mainly about what they had been through and the fact that they could actually be the last people alive which was an ever-daunting but easily discussed thought. Despite the looming end of humankind though the mood was great between them and the fact that they had all shared such horrific moments only served to make them feel closer as a group. Frank and Abbey sat hand in hand telling their stories and listened intently as Shaznay told hers, none of them wanting to miss a word and eagerly enjoying every piece of this new found social setting as it passed.

   Shaznay had heard their story of how her two new companions had met, whom they had lost and how this had all brought them together as lovers. It had been horrible to hear of their losses but the fact that they had found each other amongst this fucked up situation was amazing and she couldn't help feel happiness for them. She had just finished telling them of the group she herself had shared the theatre with and how they had left her to die on their journey to the police station. Telling the story brought the emotions rushing back as she struggled to hold back her tears of frustration at what they had done to her. The look on Abby and Frank's faces told her that she had been right to feel such hatred towards the bastards and that what they had done was beyond cowardly.

As Abbey placed a loving hand on her shoulder and reassured her that she wouldn't go through the same again it made a big difference to her, it was the simple contact and reassurance that she needed. From the short amount of time that she had already known the two of them and just the type of people they seemed, she was happy in the knowledge that she had found some true companionship amongst this hell. Companionship that wouldn't betray her and that would stay by her side regardless of how difficult or dangerous things got. She could tell already that they would make a good team amongst this mess, and who knew perhaps they would even find the elusive and perhaps non-existent rescue together.

"Thank you." Shaznay spoke as Abbey removed her hand to stifle a yawn, apologizing for the action in case it seemed in any way rude. "I will show you guys where you can shower and sleep, if you feel like me you will be more than ready for it." She continued, receiving a nod from the couple that rose from their seats and began to follow her. She led them down the corridors pointing out a few rooms of slight interest to them including the communications room where she had of course first spoken to them. She then took them to the armoury where she rustled up a man's police shirt and also a couple of the police issue vests for them to change into. "Not ideal but trust me, clean clothes have never felt better." She said passing them the items and heading off towards the shower room with them closely following behind smiling that they would soon like her look like part of a riot patrol. They arrived at a wooden door where she led them inside, she briefly showed them around and told them that she would head back to the canteen and clean up the few dishes and tins that they had used. They smiled and nodded their agreement stating that they would meet her back there once they had finished with which she turned and left them to happily clean themselves up.

The two of them showered together for almost half an hour, too tired to enjoy each other sexually the relaxation and closeness of their naked bodies was enough enjoyment to last them a lifetime. The combination of their surging happiness together and the cleanliness of the water was all that they needed at that moment in time. It felt simply perfect.

Just over a mile away a fresh fire had begun adding to the many other smoke spirals that headed skywards. This one although not directly caused by the thousands of surrounding zombies was certainly linked to the chaos as a crumbled building had ignited thanks to the electrical wires that were left dangling from a shattered wall. A gust of wind had blown these into the tattered remains of the living room curtains, which had been the simple beginning of this new combustion, which had now spread and increased quickly in size. The driver of the car that had initially ploughed into the building had died on impact and his rotten body now almost melted under the insane heat that was being produced from the raging building.

The increasing breeze was only aiding its swift and rapid movement as the neighbouring building also begun to ignite, flames licking up through the crumbling roof tiles and causing the windows to shatter outwards. It had only taken half an hour for the second building to become involved in this growing monster and it seemed that next in line was the still heavily fuelled petrol station. There were no emergency services to deal with this blaze and even the elements seemed unwilling to help as the night sky remained completely clear with not even the slightest hint of rain to come. It seemed that it was only a matter of time before the inevitable happened.

Chapter 19

Three wafer thin mattresses had been taken from within the cells and placed in the canteen and it was on these that Abbey, Shaznay and Frank now slept heavily. It had been mid afternoon by the time they had finally finished talking and let sleep take over but now the streets were dark once more and midnight approached. The tiredness that they had all felt would be more than enough for them to rest through till dawn as their bodies took the much needed time to refuel and recuperate from all that they had endured. It was the emotional aspect of everything that seemed to take its unexpected toll but this of course was understandable considering the magnitude of everything that surrounded them. After all as each day passed they were witnessing what seemed like the end of the world all around them and so far as much as they all wished it weren't so, there seemed that there was no stopping the inevitable from happening.

The explosion was quite simply phenomenal; the flames had spread to the fuel station with ease and had quickly engulfed the payment counter and the sheltering roof above the pumps. It had been the collapse of this structure that had turned a steadily spreading fire into what was now a gigantic crater surrounded by a rapidly moving inferno. The force of the detonation alone had been enough to obliterate the closest surrounding buildings however those that remained standing within a two hundred metre vicinity didn't fare any better as they were pelted with heavy flaming debris that soon added them to the list of all the other raging structures around. The heat alone from this new eruption was so intense anything even remotely flammable that lay close by was ignited instantly, the warmth from the blaze so much that the pavements had begun to crack in places along with the melting tarmac on the streets. It was devastation at its worst and it there was no immediate chance of it stopping as the catastrophe leapt from building to building in what seemed like the blink of an eye, the breeze steadily increasing and only aiding the flames on their journey as they turned everything they touched to smoke, rubble and ash.

The shockwaves from the blast had woken the three sleeping forms at the station and they had known immediately that something was seriously wrong. Every now and then since this hell had begun a tremor would be felt as small explosions kept occurring in isolated places throughout the city but this was different, it had felt massive in comparison to anything in the past even the one that Shaznay had felt on her journey from the theatre. Even through their slumber filled minds they had felt the force as the floor upon which they lay had shaken violently beneath them, some loosely stacked items toppling and smashing in the canteen that they had slept. Had they indeed been awake for the initial blast, they would have seen the window panes vibrating so forcefully that some of them had begun to crack but this mattered little now as they tried to focus and figure out what it was that had shaken them awake so suddenly and brutally.

Abbey clutched Franks arm as he headed to a window, looking out and seeing only a large handful of zombies clumsily trying to regain their footing after the shudder had left each and every one of them grounded. Apart from this though he saw nothing to explain what had just happened as he turned and shrugged at the two women behind him with nothing but a look of shock and bewilderment on his tired looking face. Shaznay glanced quickly around the room, thinking briefly before turning and running towards the door without saying a word to her companions. Abbey and Frank looked on slightly puzzled at first until they saw which way she had turned once in the corridor. Immediately her actions telling them that she was heading to the roof, which they knew, would be the most logical place to see what the fuck had just happened.

It took only a matter of moments before the three figures sprinted breathless onto the rooftop of Nottingham police station and the sight that greeted them all left them gasping and dumfounded. The entire night sky was illuminated orange and the heat that they could feel was simply insane to say how far away the blaze was. It was yet another sight that could have been dragged from their very worst nightmares but sadly they were growing used to the horrifying images that kept occurring with a frightening frequency.

"What the fuck happened?" Was the question that escaped Abbey's lips although she didn't receive an answer from her two friends who simply looked on at the madness around them in awe. In reality there was no answer to give.

She knew that they were just as clueless as her but how the hell had something like this just occurred from nothing. Had the fucking things become intelligent and grabbed hold of a fucking flamethrower? Christ, it looked like the whole fucking city was on fire and they were trapped in the bastard middle of it all. Not only that, it meant of course that this safe haven that they had struggled so hard to get to was probably no longer so fucking safe. It was with this single thought that the first teardrop rolled down Abbey's cheek and she began to sob quietly as she turned her face into Frank's chest. It was too much for her to take and the notion of having to travel through this madness once again was a hell that she did not want to even imagine.

Shaznay walked slowly and dejectedly over to the edge of the roof, all the while taking in the scenes around her and praying that the flames would stay at the safe distance that they currently were but she wasn't stupid enough to believe that her wish would come true. The inferno seemed to surround them by maybe seventy percent and she would have guessed that it was definitely less than a mile away. Unfortunately the wind that she felt on her face was carrying with it the heat of the flames, which told her everything that she didn't want to know, it was blowing the fucking blaze towards them, which would bring only one result. She simply watched on for a few minutes longer letting out a sigh as she saw one of the taller buildings in the distance collapse from the ravaging fire that had engulfed it.

She turned to the other two noticing for the first time that Abbey was crying as she began shaking her head slowly in their direction. She knew that there was no need to speak; by the simple sight of misery that stained the two figures before her she knew that they were struggling to come to terms with the simple fact that once more they would have to move on. "We need to pack." She said painfully running her hand through her hair, feeling more frustrated and angry as she had ever felt before in her life. They had fucking everything here too, absolutely everything that they needed but that mattered little now. It just wasn't fair but she knew that there was fuck all they could do about it all except to simply continue to fight on and hope that one day soon the earth would stop shitting all over them and their fortune.

As she walked past the two of them she offered a brief smile, which did nothing to comfort anyone as she headed inside to pack ready for their departure. No point in delaying the inevitable she thought as walked back inside the building. She knew that the sooner they left the better, although being eaten alive was the worst thing she could think of, burning to death did not sound much fucking better to her.

The couple had remained on the rooftop a little longer but as Frank and Abbey rejoined their friend it seemed that she had pretty much taken care of everything for them in the short time she had been inside. All the weapons and ammo were ready, food and drink too and along with this she had added blankets and pillows to the items of luggage that would accompany them on their trip. It seemed quite a lot to carry but at least it was fairly light and it would also make things more comfortable for them on the outside should they need to shelter somewhere uncomfortable. The fact that you could fit enough items to sustain an army into the police bags made life that little easier too.

"Thanks Shaznay." Frank spoke softly, his hand tightly holding Abbeys as he reluctantly reached down and grabbed what looked like the heaviest of the rucksacks.

"I have split everything evenly so there is ammo, food and covers in each one. It's not the nicest thought but should one of us become separated from the group at least they would be equipped to survive." Shaznay said as she rose from the floor taking another bag and handing it to Abbey who had now thankfully calmed down a little and begun to accept the situation that they faced. The mood amongst the trio was so low now that speaking was at an all time minimum but that was to be expected, they all knew that time could not be spared and that they just had to face the facts and once again the outside world.

Frank begun to walk, taking the lead followed by Abbey who still held his hand and Shaznay took up the rear as they unbolted the door and opened it slowly onto the street. There were members of the undead roaming all around but this had been expected and thankfully none of them were yet close enough for any concern. As the now heavy wind blasted them for the first time Abbey asked which way they were heading realising that they had not yet spoke about what they would do once outside.

"We head south, no point going back the way we came." Frank answered her squeezing her hand at the same time to offer some reassurance to the situation although knowing that his action probably did little in the way of comfort.

"Then it's lucky for us the fire is mostly north guys." Shaznay added as she began to walk toward the street that would lead them to the back of the building. She started looking around at the ash that now fell thickly like a blanket of snow making the bizarre scene in the city centre even weirder and more surreal than it had done at any point so far. "Like fucking zombie-land at Christmas." She spoke aloud smiling crookedly at the extraordinary scene around, catching one of the large grey flakes on her hand as she did so.

As they walked, each of them had their weapons at the ready, Abbey taking a shot at one of the stumbling cadavers more out of frustration than necessity as she watched it's cheekbone explode as a result.

"Nice shot." Shaznay said with a smile finding that one of the fuckers taking a shot to the face seemed to randomly lift her mood somewhat. Anything that would help to keep moral high though she thought, knowing that they now faced a long trek ahead of them as well as God only knew how many zombie encounters. Once again they would try and find any form of safety all the while knowing that the inferno followed them and that the creatures around wanted their flesh. Having seen the size of the blaze, it didn't take much for her to figure out that they would have to flee the city before they could even begin looking for another place to call home which would be the plan of action for now as they rounded the corner and looked down the long main road ahead of them. This would be the stretch of road that they would follow for now, and as expected it was teeming with hungry rotting corpses.

"When there is no more room in hell, the dead shall walk the earth"
Dawn of the Dead 1978

Chapter 20

Heading North through the city, the way that they had planned had no longer been an option. They had known that fire was capable of spreading fast but at the rate it had moved all around them they could never have imagined. It had been utter madness and the worst thing had been that they simply had no choice but to accept the fate and direction that this blaze had chosen for them. There had been only one remaining route for them which had taken a lot longer than they would have liked as they now finally neared ever closer to the M1 motorway. Although they had eventually reached their goal that was able to lead them in all directions they had wasted a lot of time and energy in avoiding the raging flames. Even the sewers had not been an option for them, the many blazing buildings collapsing from the heat and in some cases destroying the roads beneath them.

The giant orange glow of Nottingham and whatever surrounding areas had been engulfed in the blaze thankfully now seemed to be fading into somewhat of a distance behind them. On tired legs they still tried their best to reserve ammo by dodging the spaced out zombies that they passed rather than pumping them all full of hot lead which without beheading the creatures was in the grand scheme of things quite pointless. So far, the trip although long and tiring had been safe enough considering the fact that fatal danger lurked pretty much everywhere that they travelled. They had managed to avoid most attacks and those that had been unavoidable had been dealt with easily thanks to the small arsenal that they had carried between them. They had sufficient ammo to last them quite a long time but still the group knew it was much better to save as much as they could, after all they had no idea what was ahead or how long it would be before they found more bullets or weapons. The chances of them stumbling upon another unlocked, fully kitted police station were certainly slim if not non-existent.

It had been about five hours since they had first left the station as they finally reached the widespread tarmac that would if need be lead them all the way to Leeds or London. The sight that greeted them on the motorway itself would normally have brought tears to even the strongest person's eyes but the trio simply accepted the horrific vision as a simple part of what the world now was. Hundreds of vehicles lay unmoving, some upright, some on their rooftops and some simply burned to a crisp.

The twisted shells were just another hellish image that would scar their already imprinted brains but they faced no other choice than to let it wash over them and they're already tainted and darkened minds. Amongst this destruction were of course members of the undead along with so many carcasses that had been eaten before they had chance to turn into one of the monstrosities. It was a sight straight from the worst nightmare possible but so was everywhere and everything else that the three of them happened to look at, they might as well have been walking in the bowels of hell itself. The group stood for what seemed an age simply staring at the eight lanes of unmoving traffic before one of them finally spoke to break the pause that had begun.

"Anyone else peckish?" Frank said with a grunt as he threw his boot into an oncoming zombie smiling as he sent it toppling over the bridge railing into some bushes some thirty feet below. He turned with a slight grin on his face noticing that the two girls were nodding in agreement to which he responded simply by pointing to a large truck about two hundred yards down the ramp and to their right. Noticing the ladder on the back they all approached knowing that sitting atop of the stranded vehicle would leave them quite safe from attack while they refuelled their bodies and tiered minds. Being able to sit and rest would also do them the world of good, after all they had been walking and dodging attacks for a long time now and their feet needed a well deserved break.

A crowd of maybe twenty cadavers had gathered beneath them groaning and lustfully and grabbing skywards, wanting nothing but the warm flesh of those that they could not reach. Thankfully as the group atop the vehicle had known the fuckers couldn't climb, they even found it difficult enough to navigate their way around even the simplest of obstacles, which meant that they had not become mobbed by the bastard things in the time that they had been stationary. It was still quite amazing to the group of survivors that these stupid creatures had managed to destroy everything around them. There were certainly plenty of them dotted around the motorway as they had expected but there were so many abandoned vehicles that quite a lot of the zombies had become boxed in, unable to muster the simple intelligence to open a door or climb over the vehicles that hindered them. This spectacle alone had brought amusement to the trio which had been well needed to lift their depleted moods after being forced to leave the station that they had hoped so much would have stayed their home. It wasn't to be though and watching these stupid creatures bouncing angrily off the sides of parked cars, vans and trucks had at least been enough to give them a laugh while they ate their mixtures of cold tinned food and chocolate.

It had been roughly an hour since they had stopped and they knew that the longer they remained stationary the longer it would take them to find somewhere safe and dry for them to sleep and hopefully find help. It was now light enough for them to travel without the worry of things hiding in the dark although through the darkness, the illumination that had once been Nottingham had certainly helped their visibility.

It was with a groan and a look across at the gigantic plume of smoke that still rose skywards that Abbey released Frank's hand and rose to her feet. "So, we sticking with south then?" She asked, kicking her empty can of ravioli onto the wailing figures below and watching as it bounced off the face of one grotesquely disfigured zombie.

"Let's stick with south." Was the simple answer she received from Shaznay as she also stood followed by Frank who glanced around at the surrounding pack before drawing his gun ready to clear the path. The two women followed suit and with that they all begun to pump rounds into the zombies below, the skull shots grounding the monsters immediately and keeping them immobile at least for the short time it would take the trio to escape. It took them less than a minute before all of the creatures lay twitching on the tarmac as Abbey, Frank and Shaznay quickly clambered down and jogged southwards for twenty or thirty yards to give them at least a safe distance between them and their enemy. Although each and every one of them had just been shot in the head or face it certainly wasn't enough to stop them from rising again so the safety precaution was a necessity to avoid any chance of further confrontation. As they regained their breath from the short sprint and looked ahead it was apparent that their trip would be hard going that was for sure.

A lot of the cars blocking their way would have to be climbed over as the sheer volume of them made walking around impossible although this did bring the bonus of fewer zombie attacks that they would have to face. The vehicles were truly everywhere the eye could see, blocking the hard shoulders, in some cases the central reservation and pretty much any other surface that they could have walked on. It was still a shit situation that they now found themselves in and as they continued on their journey and looked at the sign to their left explaining exactly how far away they were from neighbouring cities they realised that they had pretty much no idea which way they were heading or indeed which way would be in any way beneficial. South had been the only answer that they had reached so far and this would have to do for now, it was pointless picking a destination, after all everything had probably been taken over by these bastard things anyway so they would simply walk on and hope to all the higher beings that they stumbled on anything that could fucking help them.

The flames had begun licking the outside of the building, the few windows in contact with the fire heating quickly towards the point of explosion. The station was one of few building left untouched although this would not be the case for long as it stood deep in the centre of the rapidly spreading inferno. Inside the building everything thankfully remained deserted. Apart from the furniture and machinery it was entirely uninhabited only the roaring of flames echoing throughout the many rooms. The first window to give in to the licking flames was that of the communications room. It took only seconds before the blinds and windowsills ignited, the hungry fire working its way upwards towards the ceiling and beginning to spread on the carpeted ground below. With a hiss, the fire system turned on, jets of water spraying from the ceiling as the fire alarm struggled to make itself heard over the noise of a city centre burning to the ground. As the seconds passed so the fire grew and took over the room, its heat so immense that nothing could withstand it. Ignoring the ineffective water gushing from above it slowly moved its way towards the large communications machine that had been used not so long ago by the trio that had intelligently made their escape. It was seconds before the heat caused a massive system malfunction that the gauges flicked a few times to their right and a solitary voice came through the speakers only to be unheard and drowned out by the raging inferno.

"Mayday." Was the single word that would forever remain unheard, and then once again there was nothing but the sounds of roaring fire.

Chapter 21

She was sobbing quietly; trained to be a bloody killer fair enough but in this situation she had broken down and let her emotions finally get the better of her. Naomi Sharpe sat huddled under the table, the radio transmitter gripped tightly in her hand that shook rapidly through fear, tiredness and God knew only what other emotions. It had been forever since she had been all alone, at first there had been other members of her squadron but that novelty hadn't lasted long. They had all been sent into the capital to try and restore order, hah! What a fucking joke that had been. Why try and restore order in the capital when the rest of the country had faced the exact same fucking problem. Just as it had everywhere else, the virus or plague had taken over the capital in the blink of an eye, the emergency services unable to find any form of solution to the mass attack from the ever-increasing army of zombies. The call that Naomi had received along with her seven team members had been heart breaking for each and every one of them. It had been a fucking suicide mission, plain and simple but being part of an elite armed force unit they had faced no choice but to obey.

Choppered into the hell zone, the horror had been fucking everywhere around them. Within seconds of hitting the ground they had been simply overrun, not just by zombies but by those poor bastards trying to escape from the plague that seemed to be devouring everything it touched. Three members of her team had been bitten before they had even settled on the tarmac and the rest were faced with no choice but to start firing at anything that ran or walked towards them, human or infected. The helicopter itself never stood a chance of leaving the ground again, the pilot had been unable to take off properly due to the extra weight of what looked like a hundred desperate people trying to climb on board. It had risen maybe thirty feet before he had eventually lost control and the aircraft had begun to shake violently from side to side. Bodies that clung on for dear life were shaken free, plummeting toward the gnashing teeth below whereas those that managed to retain a tight grip didn't fare any better. Seriously overloaded with weight, Shane Hannigan, had been powerless in his attempts to keep the flight stable leading only to the devastating results that had followed. After veering from side to side, the rear end of the craft sunk suddenly downwards the rest of the chopper following, picking up an unbelievable amount of speed in its decent to the street below. The remaining team saw the accident coming and dived desperately into the smashed doorway of a small electronics shop, luckily for them missing the gore filled result that occurred only fifty feet away from where they sheltered.

The spinning rotors shredded a group of almost forty people and zombies directly beneath the chopper and those lucky enough to miss the circling blades were simply obliterated by the explosion that followed. Within the confines of the store, the four armed men and women that had been lucky enough to survive were showered with glass and shrapnel, Tom, the commander being unlucky enough to take a fist-sized shard of metal to the side of his throat. Naomi had held the wound as tightly as possible but nothing she had done stopped the pumping crimson from leaking through her fingers as she had watched him quickly die in her grasp.

The whole situation had become way beyond their control in the space of a heartbeat, the sheer magnitude of the plague quickly becoming a reality as they struggled to survive through the horror all around them, unable to comprehend the extent of danger that they faced. Trying to regroup within the small store had been yet another choice that had only worked against them, a swarm of the dead coming through both the front and back of the building leaving them with the only choice of fighting for their lives. It had been at this point that the remaining team had been eaten alive, the screams of her friends still fresh in Naomi's mind although she knew deep within that it was something that she would never be able to forget. As the swarm of corpses had reached them and the painful shrieks had begun she had been pushed by grabbing hands causing her to dive blindly backwards away from the creatures that had wanted her blood. It had only been fortune that had caused her to survive as her flight took her through the only remaining window intact and back onto the street outside, luckily her landing place devoid of the many zombies. As she had scrambled to her feet and looked at the massacre that had been caused by the explosion in complete horror she had felt the tears rising within, a fear and emotion gripping her like nothing she had ever felt before. Although it tore her apart knowing that some of the shredded human remains had been innocents she had known that because of this giant loss of life she had stood at least a slim chance of escape. The hour following her exit through the store window was a complete blur in her memory now. All she knew was that she had run further and faster than she had ever done before finally stopping as she felt her consciousness waver through sheer exhaustion.

Her entire body had been saturated with sweat and shakily she had vomited next to the road sobbing through the mixture of tiredness and sorrow that she had felt. It had been there in the very same spot she had emptied the contents of her stomach that she had seen the little corner shop which she had eventually entered and searched, unbelievably finding it to be uninhabited and still reasonably stocked with food and drink. It was this very same shop where she now still remained although she couldn't help but wonder how much longer she would last within the confines of the small building.

Her food was limited in variety but sufficient to stretch over a longer period providing she continued to ration well and thankfully the water supply was as far as she knew ongoing as the taps still worked fine. She still had ten mags for her assault rifle and three boxes of bullets for her magnum, choosing to reserve her ammo rather than taking shots at the passing creatures through the windows as this seemed like the smart thing to do despite the urge to kill as many of the fucking things as she could. It was even though Naomi had a stock pile of food, drink and weaponry that she still felt a massive urge to take her chances outside amongst the stumbling corpses, the simple will for human contact rising with every day that ticked agonizingly by. She knew it had now been months since she had last seen human life and the solitude alone was what kept eating away at her fragile and frightened mind. She simply couldn't take the loneliness anymore and the thought that she may be the only remaining survivor was becoming too much too handle, she just had to find out for certain. The complete radio silence didn't help her thoughts either, by now she had issued at least a hundred distress calls each and every day, all of which remained and continued to be unanswered. With every single demoralising attempt she felt the tiny bit of positive attitude that she had left disappearing along with her strength and hopes of survival.

Thanks to this, Naomi now knew that if she remained in the store, she would not even stand a chance of finding any other living being which was the simple most daunting thought of all. She just had to decide if the search for survivors was worth dying for or if her nothingness of a safe existence was worth continuing until she eventually did run out of food leaving her to starve to death. Either way she knew her long-term future was pretty fucked up but how she was supposed to make this life risking decision she had no fucking idea. She wiped the tears from her cheeks and gritted her teeth so tightly her jaw hurt, somewhat angry at herself for crying as she mentally told herself to get a fucking grip. She sighed heavily and forced a smile telling herself that it was time to be positive as she shakily removed a pound coin from her pocket. "Heads I stay, tails I go." She whispered noticing how much this huge decision was making her feel sick. It was with a second huge sigh and the thought of fuck it that she thrust her thumb upwards and sent the coin spiralling into the air in what seemed like slow motion to her. In just a few moments Naomi would know her fate.

Chapter 22

"What the fuck!" Were the words that escaped both Frank and Abbey's mouths as they looked at the gaping hole that as far as they knew could be never-ending in depth. It had devoured at least a seventy foot piece of motorway and looking at the scorch marks surrounding the chasm it had been thanks to some kind of massive explosion although the cause of which was in no way obvious to them as they looked on in awe. No cars stood in the surrounding area, the closest vehicles had seemingly been thrown by the force of whatever had happened here, their metal frames twisted and warped from both the heat and the impact itself. Due to the untouched grass ridge to the left of what had been the road thankfully for the group it did not stop their progress however they could not help but pause and stare at this spectacle that lay before them. It looked like a scene taken from a film rather than something that could happen in life but the trio know yet again that it was as real as it could possibly be.

Shaznay walked forward and took a few steps past the couple that stood in a sideways embrace, wanting to take a closer look at the chasm, her curiosity getting the better of her as she came within less than a foot of the massive drop. She couldn't help but feel drawn to this spectacle that had her entire attention glued to its dark depths. It was simply bottomless, so dark that seeing the foundation was a simple impossibility as she kicked at a loose rock wanting to know how long it would take to make a sound of impact. It was as her leg remained outstretched and she watched the small rock fall into oblivion that the hand reached up and grabbed her. It was a slow movement however with her sights glued to the falling stone she never saw it coming, she was unprepared and taken by complete surprise. By the time she felt the clammy grip slip onto her ankle it was too late for her to react to what was happening, a scream being the only response that she could offer. Shaznay felt only an utter sense of fear as she felt gravity take hold of her body, her feet sliding towards the oblivion below thanks to the rotting remains of the decapitated zombie that had latched onto her outstretched limb. Desperately her hands clutched and grabbed for anything to stop her fall as she begun hearing the shrieks of her friends, feeling only dirt and rubble slipping between her fingers as her rapid decent continued. It was as the acceptance of death swept over her and her attempts to grab a hold of anything stopped that the inevitable fall to her death suddenly halted as abruptly as it had begun.

The cold air that had begun rushing upwards only a couple of seconds before had suddenly ceased as she hung suspended over the blackness her breath coming in short gasps as she dared not move in any way should her fall to the death continue. Scared shitless but delighted for her survival at the same time Shaznay's eyes darted back and forth for an answer as to why she was still alive, her heart threatening to break through her ribcage thanks to its rapid powerful beat. The first thing her eyes settled on was the cause of her fall, the half eaten figure lay trapped under a pile of tarmac unable to move anything but its arms and head. Still though the fucker tried despite the impossible distance to grab and bite at her warm flesh, its one and only instinct burning strong as it tried relentlessly to reach her, its decayed jaws snapping furiously. She continued her search but still nothing answered her question as to what the hell had stopped her until she slowly reached back and felt the cold metal bar that had miraculously slid underneath her police vest causing her current puppet like suspended state.

It seemed the shortest piece of shrapnel had saved her life although this was providing she could climb back up to the road and didn't plummet into the darkness in her attempt at getting back to her feet. She could just make out her two companions walking quickly but cautiously over to her, Frank immediately lying on his stomach knowing that he had to reach her quickly. She smiled nervously as she reached up, her whole body beginning to feel cold which she knew was the shock of what had just happened beginning to kick in and affect her nervous system.

For the first time as she felt Franks hand slide over hers she realised just how much she wanted to live, despite how fucked up the world was she wasn't ready to die and she prayed that he would have the strength to rescue her safely. God she was frightened. She felt his grip tighten and then with what felt like a super human strength he pulled, grunting from the exertion as he put everything he had into the movement. She felt the metal unhook itself from her vest and then in a flash she was unbelievably back on solid ground once again, safe and sound as she felt tears rush forward before she had chance to even think about holding them back.

She turned and hugged Frank immediately, sobbing almost uncontrollably as she did so knowing that if he hadn't been there she would have most certainly died. "Thank you, thank you, thank you." She cried as she looked up and smiled at Abbey too, just grateful that she had found these two people that unlike her previous companions would actually stick around to save her life. It was as Shaznay locked eyes on Abbey that everything changed in a single second. Her heart beat rose once again and the fear came flooding back as her mind processed what her eyes were seeing.

Fifty seconds beforehand, as Frank had pulled Shaznay back to safety the tangled wreckage of a minibus that clung burned to the central reservation had broken free. Without the handbrake in place and on a downhill slope the weight of the vehicle had finally become too much for it to remain in place as it had begun slowly at first rolling towards the trio that stood five hundred yards away. It was the end of this vehicle's journey that Shaznay now witnessed but unfortunately for her Abbey remained completely oblivious to the free rolling bus. By the time it hit her, the vehicle had reached almost forty miles per hour.

"I knew it would be fucking tails." Naomi said aloud to herself as she looked at the unmoving pound coin on the floor next to her feet. She knew that she didn't have to accept the decision of the coin but she had been arguing this choice for weeks now, it was time to stop the bullshit and she knew it. The longer she remained cooped up in the tiny store the worse things would get, on top of that she knew her sanity would eventually wave goodbye leaving her not just alone but crazy too. At least for now she was just alone although finally leaving this place she would at least try and put an end to that misery. She just hoped that someone else was out there somewhere, although being honest she had no fucking idea what to expect or where to start once she ventured outside.

It was with a sigh that she finally rose, knowing that she was about to go through with what the coin had told her to do. Food supplies had been packed weeks ago in the worry that she would someday have to leave in a hurry and she was certainly armed up to the teeth. There was truly nothing left for her to do but face whatever lie in waiting on the outside world. She just hoped it did not involve death or being bitten by one of those things. Despite not needing to, she reached down and retrieved the coin smiling as she did so. "If I die you shiny little bastard I will blame you." She said before pocketing the item, feeling slightly upbeat about what she was about to do but at the same time terrified. With a shaky hand she reached forward and unlocked the door. No point in hesitating, it was time.

Three shots fired and three grounded zombies were the result of her first moments outside as Naomi looked all around her to take in her surroundings and any signs of attack or danger. The monsters were certainly well spaced out which made things easy for now as she began walking cautiously back the way she had first come since she had entered the capital. She hoped that if there was help to be found anywhere it would be in the centre of London although she did accept the fact that this would also be the most zombie populated area too. Not only this she had seen firsthand how bad one area of London was so she accepted that there would probably only be danger and misery to be discovered on her journey.

It was a tough shit situation which she had no choice but to accept as she walked quickly in the directions that took her away from the wailing cadavers wondering how long before she walked past the area where they had landed together as a squadron. The thought still pained her although she had faced more than enough time alone to cope with and accept the grief that that God-awful day had brought. To this day she still couldn't believe that they had been sent in on such a fucking suicide mission but it was way too late for anything to be done now, she was simply left with the horrifying memories of what had happened.

As she sidestepped a legless corpse that was hungrily reaching for her she glanced across at a children's playground, instantly sickened to see the blood stained apparatus that filled what would have once been a place of joy and laughter. Everything she seemed to lay her eyes on saddened her and seemed to remind her of a part of her life before this horror had happened.

The fact that she had been trying for a child with her husband before all this was a thought that she had managed to completely suppress until just now as she began to wonder for the first time in an age if there was any chance he may still be alive. Until now she had ignorantly ignored the thoughts of him that had tried to surface, finding it easier to hide from the fact that he was probably deceased. She knew of course that the odds of him having survived were probably more than a million to one and there was the fact that she had no way of knowing what had happened to him. Ted was an architect and had been in Scotland unveiling a project when everything had begun to go wrong. She had not spoken to him since the evening before the first zombie reports and as the weeks had flown by since then she had begrudgingly made her peace that unless some form of miracle occurred she would probably never speak to him or even see him again.

As a solitary tear rolled down her cheek, Naomi shook herself mentally knowing that there was fuck all she could do and that getting emotional would probably cost her everything while she stood amongst the plague ridden army. She had known before leaving the store that she would see things that would be unimaginable and she knew that she just had to suck it up and deal with them, there was simply no other choice. She stopped walking for a moment and glanced around, taking aim and pumping a bullet into the cranium of the closest zombie, enjoying the thud as its body flew backwards onto the pavement. She was happy that she had a minute of safety now as she reached into her pocket and retrieved a pack of Marlboro's.

She lit one of the cigarettes, took a drag and smiled as she exhaled the plume of blue smoke. She had never smoked in her life until about two months ago, locked in the store alone but now she understood why smokers used them as a stress relief although out of everyone in mankind's existence she was quite sure that she had the best excuse of anyone to start the bad habit.

Taking one more look around she had probably covered half a mile by now and so far she was happy that it had been pretty uneventful. She would take this lack of stress and attacks any day although she wasn't naïve enough to think it would always be like this as she continued to journey on. As another zombie begun its shuffle towards her, she continued towards the capital knowing it was not the wisest idea to remain stationary for too long. It was as she rounded the next bend onto a new stretch of road that she saw it in the middle of the road, a slight excitement rising in her but knowing that the emotion was more than likely premature. Shining and seeming to call to her was a racing bike and if her eyesight was indeed correct the keys were still in the ignition.

Chapter 23

After the helpless screams, they had remained glued in position for an age, a silent embrace all that they had in response to what had just torn through their lives and their spirits. No tears came through the simple shock and horror at what had just occurred, the entire incident passing in the blink of an eye in a surreal moment that they were powerless to counteract in any way. Of all the dangers that surrounded them she had been taken in the cruellest manner possible, fighting through so much, dealing with the loss of her family, finding Frank and their new found passion only to be taken like this.

It was just impossible for the two remaining survivors to accept, she was gone, just like that, not even taken in a moment of battle or fighting for her existence. It was so unfair. Shaznay and Frank were hurting so much, unable to take this blow finding all that they could do was hold each other and somehow try to swallow what the fuck had just happened. In addition to this, the approaching cadavers informed them that through their grief, staying put was simply not an option. They would indeed have to simply deal with this horrific turn of events and push on with their own survival regardless of how difficult it felt.

The impact of the vehicle had been devastating and had most certainly killed Abbey on collision. The thud of metal on flesh had been a sickening sound, as the careering vehicle had sent this poor woman hurtling into the oblivion of the hole. It was unfortunately the last memory that they would have of her and yet again it was just another cruel twist that this new world had thrown their way.

As a groan invaded their ears, close enough to make them turn towards the source of the noise Frank rummaged in his bag and retrieved one of the grenades, his gaze never leaving the zombie that was only thirty paces away. "I know it doesn't change anything but I need to." He spoke, his voice wavering from the stress and hurt of what had just happened to his lover less than fifteen minutes before. Shaznay didn't respond, she simply took his hand and walked to the closest car so that they at least had cover from whatever shrapnel flew their way.

She herself was devastated about what had happened so she could only imagine how he must have been feeling about it all. She had already told herself that over the days directly ahead she would make sure that she kept an eye on him to ensure his emotions didn't take control and leave him vulnerable to the danger that lurked everywhere around them although seeing how strong he was she knew he would fight his way past what he was feeling, after all he had no other choice apart from giving up completely.

Once they were safely in place, Frank immediately pulled the pin and rolled the explosive in the direction of the groaning monster before taking a seat on the ground next to his only remaining friend and survivor. The few seconds passed by before the eruption rang out and rumbled the ground on which they sat, both of them jumping from the crack that still managed to take them somewhat by surprise. The car behind which they hid clanged and smashed loudly as it was peppered with shrapnel, the bodywork and windows taking on massive damage from the violent barrage. A couple of seconds later, there was silence followed by a large chunk of flesh that came thudding down only feet away from where they sat telling them that the grenade had most certainly accomplished its task.

Frank had of course known that it had not been this zombie that had caused her death but it mattered not at this moment in time. He just needed an outlet for his grief and his pain, however small it was, it was enough to keep his shattered mind going that little bit longer which was most certainly what counted and what was necessary. He felt now more than ever the urge to give up but as always he knew that this was simply not an option. As he felt Shaznay rub his arm in comfort he turned and smiled at her, glad that she was still here with him and accepting that despite the will to just let the bastards eat him so he could join both his deceased partner and now Abbey in the realms of the afterlife he had to carry on. Survival was still important and once again he tried to focus his mind on protecting himself and the one friend he had by his side.

"Looks like it's just you and me now chick." He said softly, rising and helping Shaznay to a standing position next to him.

"That's if I decide to let you tag along." She said, her warm smile returning as she looked over behind him pointing at what remained of the corpse that had moments ago exploded. Frank glanced over his shoulder and nodded his approval quite surprised at the destruction from a solitary explosive at the same time noting that they could come in very handy should they find themselves in a tricky situation. Accepting that it was time to move, a quick look towards the sky showed him that they had a while before sundown but they would still need to find a place to sleep or at least rest once the darkness came. After all it was a damn sight more dangerous travelling by torchlight which was a risk that was just not worth taking. With an aim to simply find shelter, and their minds reeling from their devastation yet again they began to walk.

The engine roared to life immediately and in the same instant a beaming smile emerged on her face. The fucking thing worked. It had been the last thing she had expected but in her hands she held a fully functional, fuel filled motorbike and she couldn't have been happier considering the end of the world bull shit of course. Perhaps leaving the pokey little shop was going to be a blessing after all.

She mounted the humming vehicle, loving the feeling of power between her legs as she revved the engine smiling once again at the sound that escaped loudly from the exhaust pipe. The surrounding zombies had been making their way towards her as fast as their rotting corpses would allow but that bothered her little now that she was armed with the extreme pace that the bike would allow. As and when she decided to twist her wrist on the accelerator she would be gone in a heartbeat flying past any of the stinking fuckers that tried to attack. With the manoeuvrability that the racing bike offered, Naomi hoped that veering through the abandoned cars would be quite a manageable task too leaving her current outlook a lot more positive than it had done only minutes before.

Naomi aimed her magnum at a decaying figure that had come a little too close for her liking; she looked at him for a few moments and then fired without hesitation. A loud crack erupted, the powerful handgun obliterating the monsters skull and a moment later the smell of cordite begun to invade her nostrils carried on the faintest of breezes. Naomi inhaled the odour with a smile as she placed the weapon back in its holster watching the lifeless zombie on the ground knowing that it was only temporarily out of action. It was time for her to continue her journey and thankfully she would be a damn sight faster with the transport that she had now acquired. The bike popped a wheelie as she set off quickly into a two hundred yard stretch of openly clear road, it was as she saw the sign ahead of her that she couldn't help but think, stopping the bike once again.

Less than half a mile ahead lay a t-junction which according to the sign would lead her either to the capital if she chose left or the north if she chose to turn right. Seeing this one simple sign made her think of her husband once again who she had been trying so hard to suppress from her mind. She stared at the sign, her jaw clenched as the tears begun to come once more, through sadness and frustration she simply couldn't help these emotions that flooded through uncontrollably. She knew that he would have wanted her to look after herself and find help and she knew deep within that a left turn into London centre would be the best and most logical option but she couldn't help the feeling of what she wanted to do despite this. Even though she was fucking miles away from Glasgow and pretty sure that he would be dead her heart and even most of her mind was screaming at her to take the right turn and head north.

It felt like another impossible decision to make, she had been sure of her plan on leaving the store and already in such a short time she was having a battle with herself on what to do, her common sense seemingly in a losing fight with her much stronger emotions.

As a groan erupted behind her she knew that she had to continue moving despite her predicament, she couldn't afford to let one of those things grab her. Despite not knowing what to do she didn't want to die because of her own indecisiveness, upset and confused or not she still had her own life to think of. She set off once again, slowly this time navigating through a few abandoned cars and other various items that had been thrown on the road by their previous owners. On her short trek from the store she had already passed such items as TV's, a doghouse and even a fridge freezer that had been left in the middle of the main road leaving her to momentarily wonder what its owner had been attempting during the moments of mayhem that must have been occurring. Travelling at the pace that she was on her newly found bike it took Naomi only a few minutes to reach the junction which had suddenly caused her so much thought. She didn't stop on her approach though as she made a snap decision which she knew she would probably live to regret, either way though she just had to know for sure as she leant to her right and followed the road around towards the string of motorways and other roads that would take her all the way to Scotland. She just hoped that she would get there alive and she prayed even more so that by some miracle she would find her husband Ted. Her mind was rightfully filled with doubt and she knew realistically that she would never find him regardless of whether he was alive or dead but she was powerless to fight her heart.

   She knew that were he in the same position as her then he would be doing the exact same thing, which at least allowed her to justify her actions somewhat as she begun what she knew would be a long and more than likely deadly journey. As she hit a nice unblocked stretch of road and accelerated rapidly the image of her husband's ruggedly handsome face flashed briefly across her mind. "Fuck it." She spoke loudly through the wind that hit her face, she would find him and if not she would certainly die knowing that she had tried. He was worth dying for.

   A long time had passed now, she could only guess at how many hours but she knew for sure that it was time to stop and call it a day. Her backside was numb, her wrists ached and she just felt drained from constantly having to be aware of absolutely everything around her. Despite her tiredness though she had found her trip so far slightly better going than she had hoped hitting only a few tricky spots where the roads had been so blocked she had been forced to dismount and walk. She had managed to reach the M1 which at least filled her with confidence about her progress so far, the road would take her most of the way north and on top of that she should be able to use either the hard shoulder, the many slip roads or even the grass verges to keep going by bike and get to her destination as fast as humanly possible. At the moment she guessed it would take her two or three days to reach Scotland which was ok although given the choice she would have much rather have been there sooner.

She had spotted the petrol station ahead, crammed with vehicles and the usual sights of decay and destruction that the plague had brought with it. She just hoped that there was somewhere she could hold up for the night without risk of her been attacked or eaten which she knew could be easier said than done. She had passed slowly by a KFC fast food restaurant and a Starbucks coffee shop on her way into the service station looking at the bloodstained logo of the Colonel sadly thinking momentarily of how many happy children and people would normally be associated with the food chain.

Not only that, the thought of a tower burger or simply some hot freshly cooked food made her mouth water and long even more for this fucked up nightmare to end although she accepted that these thoughts were certainly just a dream. She did not have to stop though as she passed by, both of the buildings were massively compromised and offered no form of safe shelter which was easily visible from the outside. This fact alone now left her with only two options, a toilet or the petrol station its self. As she approached with caution she just hoped that indeed one of the remaining places would offer the safety that she sought, her tiredness weighing heavily on her mind and body as she blinked rapidly in order to keep her concentration heightened.

Two hundred yards ahead stood the petrol station and to its right hand side the small toilet block, which she assumed, would have been left open for anyone or anything to enter as they pleased. After all these places were usually open day and night which gave her little urge to check out the rest rooms first aiming her directly at the larger of the two buildings. As she rounded a few groaning figures the first clear view of the petrol station was not the most promising one though as she noticed the devoured bodies on the forecourt and a gaping hole where a door should have been. This told her immediately that she could not expect to sleep here although there was still the hope of a store room or something else within the small shop that she could already see housed two stumbling corpses within. She stopped the bike twenty yards or so away from the entrance happy that she had sufficient time to dismount and ready herself for what attacks were possibly to come. She quickly placed her bag on the ground, slightly stretching as she did thanks to the numbness from being seated for so long before unslinging her assault rifle ready for the two fuckers inside and any other of the bastard things that happened to get in her way. As she stepped into the store the stench of the two creatures made her cringe immediately, God the level of which she despised these things was beyond any form of description. It was with a feeling of happiness and satisfaction that she took aim and applied pressure with her trigger finger. It took less than two seconds and ten shots for the powerful weapon to rip the staggering corpses to shreds.

Chapter 24

He awoke as he always did, almost jumping from his slumber to check his surroundings immediately focussed on only one thing, which was their general, safety. Thankfully the cab of the truck they had chosen had been as they had thought pretty much impregnable to the zombies. This simple bliss was thanks only to the fact that it was out of the cadavers reach. The truck was completely surrounded by abandoned vehicles, most of which luckily happened to be vans and other trucks meaning that any of the monsters close by simply did not have the basic agility and coordination to get anywhere near it. They had considered sleeping in shifts once they had decided that the lorry was the best place for them to rest but had eventually decided that it would be safe enough for them to both to grab forty winks at the same time.

After all even if the fuckers did manage to navigate their way through the obstacles and over a few car bonnets they still would have faced a mighty challenge to climb up to the cab and break in through a locked door. Despite their strength in numbers and the deadly bite that they carried, it was still a fucking Godsend that these bastard things had zero intelligence as a solitary weakness. The two survivors had momentarily wondered why the driver had at some point chosen to leave the fortunate safety that the vehicle offered although saying that they had accepted that his loss had been their gain.

Once inside the vehicle Frank and Shaznay had spoken little but arm in arm they had simply drifted into the bliss of unconsciousness where at least for a while they were free from the horrors that they had faced earlier in the day along with the many terrors that they otherwise had to deal with. It was thanks to this day-to-day stress that they had to endure and also the tragic death of their friend that they had both found their slumber to come quite easily and quickly. Exhaustion and emotional strain simply taking over, outweighing the usual fear that kept them awake every night since the death had come to the world.

Frank looked outside and as they had predicted on the previous night, the zombies seemed to have remained exactly where they had left them. He scratched his almost bearded face and yawned grumbling a little at the fact it was raining outside. Like shit wasn't bad enough he had thought on realising that the weather was also against them but he supposed in the grand scheme of things he could have woke up to a lot worse waiting outside than a little bit of typical English drizzle. He looked down at his lap where Shaznay lay still sleeping soundly and smiled to himself at her peaceful image. She was a strong young lady that was for certain and he could only be happy to have her by his side although this brought the many hurtful thoughts flooding through as he thought of those he wished were also still with him on this awful journey for survival.

So far everyone he had known and loved, whether it be from before or after the world turned on its arse had died but then again he thought it must have been the exact same scenario for Shaznay. With the saddening images floating around in his mind, a few tears escaped his eyes before he managed to mentally crush these thoughts, were he to give in to them he feared he would lose both his strength and will to carry on forward but not only that he knew that by now he must have held back enough tears to flow for a lifetime. He knew for certain that now was not the right time to release them. As he managed to stop the short flow and his emotions began to slowly subside he felt the cravings for a cigarette and shockingly it was the first time he had felt this urge in what felt like an age.

He knew he still had some in his backpack but through everything that had happened he had pretty much managed to fucking quit which given the situation was a bit of a surprise. It hadn't been through will that he had managed this though, it was much rather thanks to the fact he had been so occupied he had almost forgotten to smoke. He decided he would let Shaznay rest for a while longer though before waking her and then he would go outside for a well-deserved fag. For now though he was happy to sit and just watch the fucked up world go by, he was safe and dry and to be fair it wasn't like they had anywhere to be right now or at any time in the long foreseeable future. Looking at things realistically, he knew the chance of them finding rescue anywhere on their travels was minimal so leaving the truck was not exactly something he was in a hurry to do. Perhaps he would talk to Shaznay about staying put for a while and resting properly, perhaps she would feel the same as him about it too, they were after all safe which was a small miracle amongst the hell outside.

It had eventually been the toilets that had become her resting place for the night. After dispatching the creatures that had occupied the petrol station it had quickly become obvious that the building had been compromised and would be in no way a safe place for her to sleep or even rest for the hours of darkness. One of the main windows had been broken and besides that the mechanism for the electric door seemed to have jammed leaving a gaping hole for the surrounding zombies to enter at their leisure. On inspection, there had only been one additional room inside the small building, which had been to Naomi's dismay bolted from the other side. It had however only taken one look at the still functioning CCTV screen to see why.

One of the staff members had obviously locked themselves inside once the hell had begun and that had now sadly become their final resting place. It was a sad sight to see, someone who had simply let this tiny room become their tomb rather than face what was on the other side of the door. She had shaken her head through sadness at this image knowing that the poor man or woman who had now almost rotted to nothing more than a skeleton had remained inside and chosen the painful and dragged out death of starvation over the fear of the flesh hungry corpses in the outside world. She could hardly blame them though, the thought of giving up certainly outweighed some of the things that she had to face outside and the thought of becoming one of those things didn't even bear consideration. In all fairness, Naomi struggled to think of a worse fate than becoming one of those rotting brain dead freaks, which certainly helped her understand as to why this person had chosen to die the way that they had.

After a quick inspection, there had been nothing else for Naomi within the garage except the bathroom keys, which she had taken from behind the counter. All of the shelves had been ransacked leaving only rotten food that was of absolutely no use to her what so ever, even the chewing gum had been taken leaving her a little disappointed and deflated on her discoveries to date.

She had ventured over to the small toilet block with little expectations, knowing that it too would probably be unsafe and lurking with creatures but thankfully on her examination it was quite perfect for what she needed. With no windows, there was only one way in or out of the ladies and to her joy the door was a very sturdy one. She had disposed of the solitary creature within, dragged the corpse outside before happily locking herself inside before eating some cold beans by torchlight and then curling up on the tiled floor for some shuteye. She hadn't exactly slept well but the few hours she managed to grab within the darkness of the toilets had at least rejuvenated her somewhat ready for what she knew would be another hard day's travel in the hope of finding her husband.

A few minutes after waking and allowing her head to clear, she opened the door as slowly and as quietly as she could; now cursing the thickness and solidity of the metal. Thanks to this it was almost impossible to distinguish any sounds from outside leaving her guessing as to whether she would be knee deep in fucking cannibals on leaving the room. She held her magnum ready hoping that these primitive bastards hadn't somehow held a stakeout and waited for her to emerge back into the open although she doubted her thoughts very much as she shook her head at the notion. As the first crack of light flooded in it took her back as she blinked rapidly from the sudden pain it caused her. It had been pitch black in the confines of the lavatory and the sudden burst of daylight had took her by complete surprise as she rapidly tried to adjust her vision to accept this new intrusion. It was during these mere moments of disorientation that the two cadavers stumbled through the door knocking her to the ground and sending her gun skidding into one of the cubicles within the room.

Her head had hit the solid floor with a crack as she felt her consciousness waver heavily from the savage impact. The warm spreading feeling on her scalp informed her through her haziness that fall had cut her but she knew as she felt the clammy hands of death grab her that it was the least of her worries. She pulled her hand away looking up at the two corpses above her, the stench of decay almost unbearable as she felt both fear and disgust from the two attacking figures.

One had in life been a man, the other a woman and it certainly seemed that both had been rotting away for quite some time, their skin and flesh maggot ridden and falling away in chunks from only the slightest of movements. Their fragile nature mattered little though as they continued clumsily forward, their hands and mouths hungrily groping towards Naomi who still lay dangerously beneath them on the ground, trying with all her might to escape their clammy rotten grip. She blinked rapidly once more as she continued shuffling backwards unwilling to take her still startled gaze away from the two zombies to locate her pistol. As seconds passed, her sight begun to recuperate as she reached the far wall of the bathroom. Now unable to escape she had to face the two demons that wanted her flesh so badly.

With all her might she thrust her foot upwards, the sickening impact causing the lead creatures throat to collapse before it staggered backwards almost falling from the power of the blow. In the split second Naomi had she almost jumped to her feet, ignoring the slight dizziness that still consumed her mind as she hurriedly began to unstrap her assault rifle, which she had been unable to do whilst grounded. Struggling in her panic she had to pause with her actions in order to issue another hand to hand blow to the second creature which grasped for her face, her evasion allowing her thankfully to miss the groping limb by mere inches. She threw another kick forward this time sending the zombie hurtling into one of the cubicles, the thud of its skull against the porcelain system almost music to her ears as she continued her efforts to become properly armed. This time knowing that she had at least a few more seconds to spare she managed the usually simple task and smiled to herself as she pointed the weapon towards the male zombie that walked clumsily once more towards her. She pulled the trigger with joy and fought the violent kickback watching as this awesome weapon pretty much cut the creature in half. She turned immediately and saw that the other demon was still struggling to stand within the confines of the cubicle, which made her job to dispose of this cadaver that, little bit easier.

She walked the few steps towards the zombie and held her weapon to its rotting scalp before pulling the trigger once again, looking away to ensure she didn't get spattered from the resulting gore. She knew though that despite what she had just done, they would only be out of action for a while but that was plenty as she knelt down and peered underneath the other cubicle walls, locating her handgun without any problems. With a slight hurry in her step she retrieved the magnum before doing her best to look at her head injury in the dimly lit bathroom mirrors. On inspection, it had thankfully felt worse than it seemed, the blood flow seeming to have almost stopped although she cursed a little at the fact her hair had already become matted thanks to the crimson fluid that had leaked from the gash.

As Naomi finally stepped back outside she was happy to notice that apart from her sudden attack, nothing out of the ordinary had happened during her hours of sleep. Her bike remained where she had left it, the zombies in view were still nice and spaced out which meant all she had to do was fill up the bike and carry on her journey up the motorway. It took a few minutes at the pump and two more bullet-ridden zombies that came a little too close before she mounted the vehicle and set off once again to continue her journey. As the wind hit her face and she hit the motorway tarmac her anticipation rose, she was getting closer to her husband, her prayers for his safety growing stronger with every mile that she covered. She just hoped with everything that she had that Ted by some form of miracle had managed like her to survive this hell.

Chapter 25

The first cigarette's in an age, hadn't been as enjoyable as he thought but despite this he remained stood in the rain smoking his third of the morning, both him and Shaznay sheltering under the same coat as they looked on at the few moaning figures trapped between cars that they simply couldn't get round or over. It was quite a bizarre sightseeing these things that had taken over everything so quickly and brutally completely baffled by something so simple due to their lack of intelligence and manoeuvrable abilities.

"Can I have another?" Shaznay asked tossing her first cigarette butt into a puddle, watching the glowing orange distinguish with a slightly audible hiss. They had spoken moments before about what the plan for their immediate future was to which she really hadn't possessed much of an answer. She still wasn't sure now but she had certainly felt the same as Frank had, after what had happened to Abbey she too had little energy or motivation to move on for the time being. After all like Frank had said to her what exactly were they moving on for? Help, rescue, hope or just for something to do? They had no real idea if anyone else had survived or if there would be rescue anywhere, sure they hoped for these things but they had to accept that there could only be disappointment waiting for them.

In a way she couldn't help but think they had as much chance of being rescued simply by staying put rather than wandering around the dangerous zombie crowded streets. Whatever they did, at the end of the day they were simply hoping to find a possibly non-existing needle in a giant fucking haystack. Either way she wondered if their actions mattered but they had eventually decided rationally that there would be no harm in remaining at the truck for another day or so. The rest would certainly do them good, it would give them chance to try and refocus their fragile minds and it had the added bonus of keeping them safe from harm too. Considering all it certainly seemed like the best choice for now.

As Shaznay lit the cigarette and let the plume of smoke out with a sigh she felt franks hand gently rub her shoulder.

"Everything will be ok, I promise." She heard him say softly. She heard the doubt in his voice but chose to ignore it hearing only the reassurance that she needed for now. Despite how strong she knew she was seeing Abbey die had really rocked her system but thankfully she didn't have to pull through it alone. She at least had a true friend left in Frank; still alive with her and for that she thanked her lucky stars.

"I know it will be." She eventually responded smiling warmly and putting her hand on his. "Oh and it's your turn for breakfast." She continued sticking her tongue out and laughing at the fact he rolled his eyes on hearing the comment thankful for her efforts to lighten the continuously dull mood. Perhaps everything would be ok after all he thought to himself before turning to prepare the morning's meal for them both. They had both lost too many friends, family members and loved ones through this bull shit but they had each other which would keep them going. For the first time he felt a slightly positive edge regarding their situation, he just hoped that his outlook continued to rise. The two of them had managed to spend the first half of the day simply chatting, eating, smoking and mainly resting. For the first time in what seemed like forever they managed to forget about everything around them and somehow feel the normality of relaxation and friendship. Trapped in their protected little bubble they only needed each other's company and the few supplies they had which suited them perfectly as they laughed and joked with each other, simply loving the company that they had and managing thankfully to forget about all the tragedies that they had witnessed.

For the shortest amount of time everything seemed so much better as they simply pushed all of the evil and hurt out of their minds, although they knew that this momentary bliss would not last. Eventually they would of course have to face the world once again, every creature that walked on its surface and everything that they would more than likely throw at them. For now though they had this little Eden of theirs and they weren't about to let a few dark thoughts dampen what they had found.

After lunch, for a turn of pace Shaznay and Frank spent most of their time using the vast amounts of ammo they had for their own personal amusement. They ensured enough rounds were kept to keep them safe for the foreseeable future whereas the rest were happily used to obliterate the zombies that were within any sort of reasonable distance to their truck. The little game kept them more than amused and happy through into the afternoon before they both finally retired back to the cab for another bout of rest and something to eat. The way the both of them felt after a day of what could only be classed as luxury compared to the alternate standard of living it was hard for them to imagine leaving this place that they had found amongst the hell. Bizarrely it was the closest they had felt to home since the zombies had arrived.

Naomi had covered a lot of ground and she happily knew it. The fuel gauge was now just below half and her legs were certainly feeling the length of time she had been on the bike once again. So far during the half a day or however long she had been travelling she had only been forced to dismount twice to navigate through heavily crowded roads, which despite the cramps from constant travel had been a massive blessing. She had never thought that she would make it so far north so fast receiving only minimal hassle from the many corpses she had passed. So far she had been amazed at how little aggravation she had dealt with, managing to avoid all attacks apart from one which she admitted to herself, she had been lucky to escape from. She had tried to veer around the lunging arms of a rather overweight creature however he had manage to pull her from the bike and send her skidding along on the tarmac.

Thanks to her low speed and the wet ground the impact of her fall had been minimal ensuring she had been able to scramble back to her feet quickly before the creature could attack again. After two devastating punches to the zombie's rotting head she had been able to continue on her travels happy to see her bike had also remained intact minus one of the side mirrors. The incident could have been a lot worse but thankfully it seemed that she had come through it intact and a little bit wiser too bearing only a few bad grazes for her troubles. Since then she had however been travelling with her gun at the ready accepting that she had indeed been very fortunate and that hand to hand combat was not the safest method to deal with these things. She knew very well after all that one bite would be the end for her, which was of course the last thing she wanted having come so far in the search for her husband Ted. There was no way in hell she would let these bastards win now, as she focussed more than ever on her quest that would continue to take her north. So far she had been ignoring the thought of what she would do if her husband was indeed dead when she arrived thinking only of each step of her journey as she encountered it. The negative thoughts were simply dismissed as soon as they cropped up in her mind, her strength and will telling her instead that he was indeed alive and that she would soon be in his warm embrace. Should the worst-case scenario happen then she had accepted the fact that it would be dealt with there and then rather than unnecessarily beforehand.

As Naomi rounded a series of burned out vehicles, veering onto the grass verge to avoid a gaping hole in the motorway she couldn't help but wonder what the hell had happened to create such a massive crater in the earth. Going by the blackness surrounding everything she assumed an explosion but decided not to think too much into it, after all she needed her concentration to be focused on the fact that she could be attacked at any point especially if her concentration were to waver in any way. Looking to her left and seeing a service sign six miles ahead she decided to keep on cruising until she reached the restaurants, rest rooms and yet another petrol station. She had found somewhere to rest last time she had chosen this option so hoped her luck would continue with a second attempt. Providing her journey continued at the pace it had all day she hoped to easily reach her stop within an hour, two at the very most. Unbeknown to her though it would only be another mile directly ahead until she reached two other survivors.

She was hearing things, she was sure of it. Laid with her head on Frank's stomach she struggled through her sleep filled mind to concentrate on what she was sure sounded like an engine. She lifted herself to a seated position groaning a little as her elbows cracked from the movement as she peered out through the front window of the truck unable to see anything but a couple of cadavers that had made their way closer since she had last been awake. Shaznay rubbed her eyes and stretched all the time listening to the noise that not only still existed, seemed to be growing louder with each second that ticked by.

A flutter of excitement registered within as she looked at Frank who still slept heavily, his eyelids twitching rapidly indicating he was stuck in the realms of dreamland. She wondered whether to wake him but decided momentarily against it wanting to find out for sure if there was any news to tell him rather than get his hopes up for nothing. As she craned her neck to peer through the side mirror the noise had increased so much that she knew it was almost upon them and that it was most certainly a reality. It was as she opened the door the noise passed her rapidly on the opposite side to where she had begun to descend. As fast as her body would allow she leapt to the tarmac, cursing at the cold wet feeling that hit her bare feet and legs as she ran round the front of the lorry wearing only a t-shirt and underwear which was what she had slept in only moments before. As she looked forward her heart jumped into her throat as she tried to accept what was in front of her. "It's a fucking motorbike." She spoke out loud before yelling at the top of her voice to get the attention of the rider.

Screams of over here and stop came flooding from her mouth so loudly it hurt her throat as she desperately tried to make herself heard by the woman who was already a hundred yards away and only increasing the distance between them. It became almost immediately apparent to Shaznay that over the roar of the engine this woman simply could not hear her as she turned and leapt into the cab once more to see a very startled half asleep Frank. Shaznay muttered the words motorbike and survivor before reaching across and blasting the horn as hard as she possibly could, her fist repeatedly hammering the centre of the steering wheel. As she looked up fearing the distance would be too great she saw exactly what she had hoped, the bike had stopped and the woman looked confusingly back towards them trying to locate the source of the horn. As Shaznay and the still sleep ridden Frank began to wave this newcomer turned and began heading slowly back towards them. They couldn't believe it; someone else had survived through the madness.

Chapter 26

Another night had now passed and pretty much everything had been exchanged from life stories to scrapes with zombies and even chatter about the weapons that each of them now carried with them. Life had suddenly changed once again for all of them and a positive feeling surrounded the trio as they all sat on top of the truck enjoying the warm morning sun that had broken through the clouds a few hours beforehand. Despite the overwhelming will to find her husband the simple human contact that she had now found had been needed badly for Naomi and like the other two she just couldn't believe her fortune at finding more survivors. She had been alone for so long in the store she had begun to wonder if her sanity would begin to slide but thankfully she realised now that she had magically avoided this seeming inevitability.

Between them they couldn't help but wonder how many more breathing people could possibly remain, having thought for long periods that they had been the country's sole survivors. Having found each other though they couldn't help but wonder if more had made it through the hell, though saying that, they wouldn't have been surprised if they were the last ones alive considering the state of everything around them.

Naomi had informed them that she had been heading north to try and find her husband and although they understood why she was doing this they had told her she would be better off staying with them for the simple safety it offered. They had also begrudgingly told her that the chances of him having survived were pretty much zero which had upset her somewhat on hearing it come from someone else's mouth but both Frank and Shaznay had thought it a necessity to put this truthful point across. Naomi of course understood what they meant and she also understood why they wanted to stay put for now but she simply couldn't and wouldn't rest until she had done what she had set out to do. She had asked them to join her journey north but Frank and Shaznay were capital bound in their own aim should they actually decide to move anywhere having found this little safe hold amongst the chaos. They did have plenty of supplies and the possible reality that there was no safety to be offered elsewhere so to be fair she couldn't blame them for staying put.

As the morning crawled by they had been discussing the future for over an hour coming to the conclusion that it was no use trying to talk the other party out of their individual decisions. It seemed each party was firmly set on their own decisions. The group had however managed to reach a compromise on what to do knowing that simply saying goodbye and going their separate ways was not a viable or intelligent option. Naomi had informed them that she would search for her husband regardless but that she would only spend a day completing this task in order to come back to them so that they could all move forward as a unit. Including the drive north and then back, she expected to be gone for four days tops which the duo who she had initially thought were a couple confirmed they would happily spend waiting at the truck until she returned. They had stressed their will for her to accept her husband was gone and that her journey was pointless and probably deadly but it had not worked in the slightest, it seemed that nothing could stop her.

It was as she took a drag on the cigarette that Shaznay noticed Naomi checking her guns and bag. "Your gearing up to go aren't you?" She said smiling as the other woman nodded immediately with confirmation to her. "I really hope you find him chick, and I mean that. You must love him so much." She continued noticing the glimmer of tears in Naomi's eyes.

"Just make sure you and your husband come back here ok." Frank interjected his voice seeming to stop the sadness that had started building for her.

"I will." Naomi responded quietly before standing and putting on her rucksack that Frank and Shaznay had kindly added food to. She was all set and ready to go and she knew that there was little point in delaying her pending journey. The longer that she waited the less light she would have to travel by which was fucking important when it came to dodging zombies on a motorbike as she had learned so far. As she clambered down to street level her new friends followed behind, Shaznay's arm draped around Franks shoulder as they followed her to the waiting motorbike yet again in what she couldn't help but think was a couple like fashion.

"Are you two sure you're not an item, cos it just seems to fit." Naomi asked grinning as she saw the two of them go instantly red at the remark, both shaking their heads furiously with embarrassment. She knew of course that Frank had just lost another woman he had been involved with in Abbey but she was simply being honest with what she had observed since meeting them. If anything it seemed to her that it was the tragic loss of Abbey that had brought these two so close and almost forced them together. "Trust me." She continued. "I know what you have been through recently but if I were you guys I would take any form of warmth, love or passion that you can amongst this fucked up mess. You guys seem like good people and whether you like it or not I can tell there is something there. Just a thought for you while I'm gone." She finished before climbing onto the machine ready to leave them pondering her comments as she smiled again at the slightly uncomfortable situation she had left the two of them in.

"One last smoke?" Frank offered which she duly accepted, knowing that he had just wanted to steer the conversation away from himself and Shaznay.

The three of them stood, enjoying each other's company for the last few minutes before Naomi eventually started the bike and with a cheerful wave slowly disappeared into the distance, weaving in and out of the many abandoned vehicles and creatures that lay in wait. She was so determined to find her husband and her devotion had touched both Shaznay and Frank, leaving them with a wonderful first impression of this woman that they hoped they would soon see again. She was a very welcome addition to their small survival group and they knew that her husband, should she miraculously find him alive, would be the same sort of person that they would happily have alongside them. Arm in arm, Frank and Shaznay continued to watch her until she was out of sight knowing that all they could do was wish her luck and prey for her survival and safe return. Neither of them could ignore the massive feeling of doubt they shared though, after all they knew exactly what it was like to try and survive alone in this hell, prepared or not, it was almost impossible.

The travelling had again been as uneventful as could be hoped. A few dismounts needed but thankfully no drama and no crashes; it had been a zombie free trip for Naomi and she could only be grateful for the blessing. She now stood stationary in front of the sign proclaiming she was about to enter Scotland and for the first time she could no longer fight the fear that she would more than likely be unable to find Ted regardless of her will and fight to do so. She would try her fucking hardest though that was for certain but now that she was so close the realisation had hit home; the chances of him being alive were pretty much next to nothing.

Naomi sighed loudly as she retrieved a crumpled cigarette from her jacket at least happy to see that it had not split as she placed the orange filter into her mouth. Ted would disapprove she thought with a grin as she lit the slender white stick and inhaled deeply. He had never liked smoking, and if he saw her with one the shocked look he would no doubt present her with would be classic. She would be able to talk him round though if that scenario ever presented its self, she knew it. He had always been a soft touch though, joking how she had him dangling like a puppet from some strings if she wanted something bad enough. The thoughts immediately made her sad although she couldn't help but smile at the thought of him; the feeling of heartache so bad she felt like her soul was slowly drowning. God she missed him so much and just wanted him with her and holding her tightly.

As she felt her will slipping somewhat, Naomi mentally tried to shrug away the mood that she didn't want to take a hold of her. She had come too far and was too close to start letting shit eat away at her knowing that now more than ever strength was a must. She knew damn well that until she found out for sure about him there was no point in getting emotional, not only would it be pointless right now but the lapse in concentration could also be deadly as she closed in on her goal. She breathed in another drag from her Benson happy that she had managed to somewhat shift her negative thoughts before looking around in all directions. The closest cadaver was a hundred yards away, which gave her plenty of time to at least enjoy the few moments rest with her fag before carrying on the last stretch of her journey. If the way ahead was as clear as the travelling had been so far, she could even make Glasgow before dark.

Chapter 27

It was nightfall again as the two of them settled into the cab, still more than content with their little haven amongst the hell. Since Naomi had left they had done little apart from venture out maybe half a mile in each direction from the truck to take care of any zombies that were even remotely close to them. They had faced enough death and shit happening to them for even any slight mistakes to be made. They had simply ensured that they would remain safe by living their lives with every bit of caution that they could. It was the only way that they could be certain to avoid the death that had taken everyone else.

Since the departure of the newfound survivor, they had also discovered a happiness that they couldn't help but welcome. It was not only for the warmth and comfort that it offered but for the simple distraction to the destruction around them too. Thanks to Naomi they had been able to look past Abbey's death and see their own connection, which was why they now lay arm in arm, their mouths locked together as they begun to enjoy each other passionately for the first time. It had felt strange for them to accept and they had also felt guilty at first but Naomi's words had been strong in their minds telling them that they should take this opportunity for happiness amongst misery. They were in their own little world and for the time being nothing mattered but them. Not the thousands of abandoned vehicles, the grey clouded sky or even the families that they had lost so quickly and brutally. It was quite simply their time at least for this night and they would cherish every single second of it, after all every day could be their last.

She had not been sure what to expect but still she was a little surprised at her own shock as she surveyed the sights ahead. It looked pretty much like everywhere else, completely fucked up beyond repair, but still she felt like the devastated image of the city centre had crushed her soul and her so far iron like will. She of course knew why she felt this way, after all this was the end of her quest. This was where her husband had been and hopefully would still be, although seeing what remained of the metropolis left her more than deflated. She had of course hoped to find Glasgow untouched by the madness but sadly it had undergone the same horrors that the rest of the country had experienced. Buildings where burning, zombies stumbled and groaned everywhere and the signs of death and massacre littered almost every inch of every street. It was a sight that certainly hit her more than she had expected it to, perhaps because it looked impossible to survive such terror she wasn't quite sure.

She knew that there was a minimal chance of finding him but she wasn't about to quit now she had come so far as she turned the accelerator once more and began weaving through the eternal traffic of abandoned cars and stumbling corpses once again. She knew without thought where the building was that he had been unveiling and that was the logical place for her to head to. She knew it was only a five-minute ride away at best leaving her almost trembling with nervousness and anticipation. She just hoped to God that she found him, dead or alive. If he wasn't there then she was fucking clueless as to what she would do in order to track him down. She just needed to know for her own peace of mind, good news or bad.

Tears had begun streaming down her face as she walked slowly up to the majestic building. It was beautiful, glistening panels of glass showing the perfection and the passion that had been put into its very five-floor creation reminding her exactly why she was risking everything to search for her husband who was most likely dead. The building seemed to personify his beauty and his personality which made her both happy and sad as she felt a crushing fear of what she may be about to find.

She pushed her way through the blood stained and cracked rotating doorway entering a lobby that despite the smell of death and decay still carried the odour of the freshly built edifice. She raised her assault rifle and rattled off a handful of shots, felling a zombie that wandered a little bit too close for her liking hoping at the same time that this creature hadn't at any point had an encounter with Ted. She looked around seeing the carnage that told a story of its own, a mass panic had quite obviously happened within the spacious room leaving behind only the most basic of human remains. These were the things that she had dreaded, her fear and anxiety rising by the second as she wiped the nervous sweat from her brow. The reception desk further on was where she headed; vaulting clumsily over the front to see if anything of any use remained for her. The drawers were empty as were the cash registers, the solitary computer screen perhaps offering a little more assistance as she manoeuvred the mouse to disable the machines standby mode.

After a robotic buzz and a hiss of static the screen blinked into life showing the silent views from a CCTV camera that by the looks of things remained pointed at a corridor from one of the upper floors. The image that she saw looked very similar to those that surrounded Naomi, simply death and nothing more as she shook her head once again knowing within that her husband would most probably have been caught up in the middle of it all. The image suddenly changed, this time showing the car park and the fact that a man with little remaining of his face and left shoulder had knocked down her motorbike with his deathly shuffles.

Naomi shook her head once again at the small annoyance and made a mental note to pump a few rounds into the fucker once she left the building. Apart from the few scratches the bike would have obtained though this bothered her little, so long as the fucking thing started that was all that mattered to her. She begun impatiently tapping her fingers on the desk as she waited once again for a new image to emerge, half wondering whether or not to begin searching room to room as finally a new picture revealed itself to her. It took a few moments to register but as she finally recognised the jacket draped over the flesh and bones within the elevator the breath simply froze in her lungs. It can't be were the words that repeated themselves over and over in her head as she frantically managed to pause the image before it changed once again. Her heart thundered in her chest and a nausea emerged in her stomach as she examined the black and white screen hoping that something would jump forward and tell her that it was in fact someone else but the longer she looked the more she knew that this wouldn't happen. The suit that she saw was the same that he had worn on leaving the house and the briefcase he carried was the one she had bought him two Christmas's beforehand. It was him, no question about it although the face that she could see hardly even resembled the man she loved. There was no doubting it though, she was staring at the image of Ted and no tears would come, she felt too devastated and heartbroken as she took two steps back. She felt the sturdiness of the wall behind her, her eyes still fixated on the flickering image of her dead husband.

She began breathing heavily, the thoughts that she would never hear his voice or feel his touch again flooding rapidly through her mind as the emotions of what she had discovered began to push their way through as a terrifying reality. Naomi slid slowly to the ground as she finally began to sob uncontrollably, until now there had always been the slight optimism that he may have survived through the horror but now all she had was the cruel fact that he was no more. The horrifying truth that her husband was dead hit her like a train as she failed with any attempt to control her feelings, just facing no choice but to let everything go. Her loud cries mingled with the groans of the dead as the two noises combined to fill the rooms within the building that her husband had designed and also died in. She was alone and she would never hold him again, her cries and tears coming so rapidly she wondered if they would ever stop.

Her head ached from the emotions and pain that she had released as she opened her tired eyes, her vision blurred at first as she recovered from sleep. Thoughts began once more to quickly tumble through her head, the upsetting discovery, the fact that she had continued crying into the night and then the horrifying thought as her sight cleared that she had obviously fallen asleep in a zombie filled building. The last thing she could remember was the inability to stop herself from crying however it had certainly been night time, now though it was the sight of daylight that greeted her along with the underside of the receptionist's desk. On sleepy legs Naomi sprung to her feet grasping for her rifle at the same time wondering how long she had slept and how the hell she was still alive after being so careless. The answer revealed itself immediately as she looked out into the lobby seeing that that thanks to the unusual height of the reception desk and the physical ability of those zombies within she had remained safe through her slumber. Ignoring the few cadavers close by she glanced painfully at the computer screen once again mouthing the words I love you before un-clicking pause on the screens menu as she watched the image of her deceased husband eventually disappear, replaced by a shot of yet another horrific image.

The next screen showed what had obviously happened in another area of the building, the giant boardroom housing dozens of corpses and even more zombies. Christ there must have been a hundred of the fuckers inside as Naomi correctly assumed this had been the initial survivors hide out within the building. It was yet another sad sight knowing that all these people had been caught up and infected while trying to hide from the plague but in a sense it made her see one positive amongst the mess. Through all the horror that had happened within the building her husband had at least manage to avoid it, he had not been bitten or eaten by these things. He had found a safe place and tried to wait for rescue, which had at least meant a form of natural death, which she hoped, would manage to give her some closure on the subject that still hurt as much as when she had first seen him the night before. She knew it always would tear her apart and that it was something that would certainly take a long time to accept but for now she knew what had to be done.

As far as she knew there were three survivors left including herself and that was something that she needed to hang on to as she prepared herself for another journey back the way she had come. Although she had not had the results she had wanted at least now she knew what had happened as she took one last look at Ted's creation feeling yet more tears flowing down her cheeks. Despite the urge to stay in the place where her husband was she knew there was no point, it was time to leave regardless of her low mood and motivation was, it was what Ted would have wanted her to do.

She wiped her face and forced through a smile, happy at least that she could still feel a slight fight to survive within herself as she looked outside to see the zombie that had knocked over her bike the previous night. "Good morning fuck face." Were the simple words she uttered as she checked her ammunition and headed towards the exit accepting the tears that still ran freely from her eyes. She was hurting inside and probably always would be but she had to accept that today was indeed a new day and she would most certainly make the most of it. She would survive.

The time that had passed since Naomi had left had been spent lazily as both Frank and Shaznay spent the time enjoying each other and the feelings that they newly shared. For now though they both grinned massively at the sight before them, surprised but ecstatic that Naomi had not only survived but also come back to them. The fact that she was alone told the couple that the search for her husband had been unsuccessful which filled them both with a sadness and sympathy for her. Ted was most likely deceased or had perhaps been turned into one of those fucking virus carriers. Either way though they would give her the support she needed and welcome her back with open arms, after all they were the sole survivors of this major catastrophe having only each other to rely on.

The two of them had been enjoying the sunshine from the roof of the truck when the faint sound of a motorbike engine had invaded their ears for a second time, both of them leaping to their feet and peering into the distance waiting for a visual confirmation of what they could hear. It had not taken long until Naomi had come into view Frank instantly climbing down behind the wheel and beginning to furiously beep the horn to let Naomi know she had made it back to them. After all there were that many abandoned trucks on the motorway, the chances of her recognizing theirs by herself was minimal to say the least as he managed to attract her attention with his repetitive honking. It took another few minutes for her to reach them and it was a happy moment for them all as they shared a group hug that lasted an age, each of them ecstatic at their reunion.

Once the group had settled back on the roof of the truck, each with a cigarette in hand they began to chat and catch up on the time that they had spent apart. At first the unpleasant news was confirmed by Naomi, yet more tears escaping as she explained what she had found as quickly as she could to avoid getting too emotional.

Her two companions offered their sincere apologies about what had happened to her husband and the fact that she hadn't discovered better news. On a brighter note she had then revealed three bottles of rum that she had discovered on her journey back down the motorway happily opening one and taking a drink before passing it on. After all, their reunion was a reason for celebration and at the same time she could at least try and forget her newfound sorrow for one day at least. She deserved that much and she certainly deserved a drink as she took another hefty swallow of the warm liquid.

For what daylight remained, the reunited trio continued to drink and smoke, once again forgetting about the surrounding hell exchanging stories and simply enjoying the little happiness that they currently had together. It was a much needed release for them, each person knowing in the backs of their mind that food supplies were starting to run low and that despite the joy and safety the truck offered they would soon have to leave. After all perhaps rescue would be waiting out there somewhere and if it indeed was, they wouldn't find it by remaining on the middle of a motorway. The fact that this haven away from the madness would have to be left behind was an acceptance that they would all begrudgingly have to make.

It was the next morning through slight hangovers that the plans were made as they shared out the last rations for breakfast, leaving only a few snacks for their travels and whatever the day ahead would hold. Thanks to Naomi they knew there was nothing in the capital and nothing as far north as Glasgow; she had seen no signs of help or safety on her travels so far allowing the group to rule out a journey in a northern or southern direction. They agreed quickly that the best form of action would be to simply head for the coast. Should England have no survivors and no form of rescue, the coast was the only way forward for them. After all France was always another option and one that they hoped would offer more success than they had found so far.

By midday the group were packed and ready to go, no real route planted in their minds, just a simple aim to escape driving them towards the deep blue. Prepared for the worst they began to walk yet again.

Chapter 28

It was hard to decide how to feel upon reaching the small docks near to the coastal town of Mablethorpe. Their travels had been expectedly tough and taxing, dodging the grotesque monsters that lined every street and sleeping in shifts had certainly taken their toll on the trio both physically and mentally. Upon seeing the ocean they had of course all been ecstatic though this elated mood had soon changed upon seeing the choice of travel they had been left with once reaching the docks themselves. It seemed that all of the boats had been taken during the plague most of which seemed to have now washed ashore to become grounded or sunk.

Bizarrely it had never crossed their minds that all the boats may have been taken but as they looked on at the lack of transport it became apparent that their choice was certainly limited. On arrival, the tide was out revealing just how many people must have tried this same method of escape but it seemed that most had failed miserably, the bloodstained vessels revealing that the cannibals had somehow made it aboard devouring the poor bastards as they had tried to flee. Either that or the fucking things could swim which was of course the most unlikely of notions considering they couldn't even walk in a straight fucking line.

It seemed though after a long search not all was lost for the group as Shaznay excitedly pointed out to sea, showing one solitary little boat bobbing along in the waves, seemingly untouched by the horror. To their luck, the vessel seemed quite reachable; easily within swimming distance, which told the three of them it was definitely worth a try and could more than likely prove to be their means of finally escaping the country that they had all once called home. This horrific place was no longer that though, too much had happened taking away all the happy memories and replacing them with a simple hatred for everything that surrounded them. They would all be happy never to see this place again and it was that thought that flowed through their minds as they contemplated what would face them on their newest journey ahead.

As they all began to walk towards the ocean, the urge for them to run out of the excitement they felt was simply huge, each member of the trio knowing though that conserving their energy was a much better option as they quelled the urge to rush towards the small boat.

"Chances are it's out of fuel, we can check the broken boats on the way though." Were Naomi's words as she begun heading eagerly down the steps towards the sand, kicking a heavily decayed zombie over the railing as she did so, enjoying the crunch of bones as it crashed heavily onto the sand beneath. Hand in hand Shaznay and Frank followed smiling at the fact their journey had now finally reached what could be a massive turning point for them all. They had after all travelled half the width of the country to get where they now were, dodging the bastard plague with every step leaving them feeling overdue a very large reward for their troubles. They could only hope and pray that it had been worth the efforts though and that this solitary floating craft would take them somewhere safe that seemed a million miles away from the memories and horror that haunted them with every step they took.

The first two boats that they checked thankfully and unbelievably both turned up three canisters of fuel leaving the group feeling for once quite fortunate and lucky. They could only hope that it was a sign of things to come although their fortune also came with various sights of gore and death upon the vessels that they had inspected. The fuel however was what they had wanted so with the cargo now in their possession they had the quarter mile or so walk out to the ocean and what they hoped would be a quick and easy swim to the boat.

It certainly didn't look far and the water seemed calm enough for them to manage leaving the trio grinning at the possibilities that could be awaiting them ahead. They all accepted that should they reach France, it could of course be in the same fucked up state, as England but that didn't extinguish the burning hope for something better. Even if it was a dilapidated fucking zombie spewing hellhole at least it was something new and fresh to tackle rather than a country that they now knew offered no form of rescue. Ideally of course on their arrival, they wanted a rescue army waiting for them, they wanted a hot bath in a luxury hotel with clean clothes and sheets, they wanted a hot meal, a cold pint of beer and most of all they wanted a life that was fear and zombie free. It wasn't that much to ask, they just hoped that it would be waiting for them on the other side of the Channel.

Frank was the first to clamber aboard the wooden boat, breathless from his exertions in the choppy water, the swim being a few hundred yards further than they had first thought taking away a lot of energy that he didn't really want to depart with. There had been a slight current against them too which they had not expected and adding this to the fact they were swimming with heavy weapons and fuel tanks it had certainly been a fucking struggle. Once he had gathered himself, he retrieved a pistol from one of the carrier bags they had used to keep the weapons dry, telling the ladies to remain in the water while he checked the hopefully vacated vessel. He hoped that he would manage his inspection without any form of confrontation, feeling ever closer to survival and also he was worried that he would be lacking in strength to defend himself from an attack.

On his first glimpse around the deck, the sight was simply devastating, making him turn away and struggle to keep back the emotions that rose instantly within. Thankfully there were no zombies but looking on at the scene that lay before him he would have probably preferred one of those hungry bastards than what he had been forced to see instead. It was what looked like a mother and daughter who had managed to flee the initial terror safely although that small bliss seemed to matter little in the grand scheme of things now that he could only see the result. All he could assume was that they had stayed on the ocean and starved to death arm in arm rather than risking a certainly painful death by returning back to land. In a sense he supposed it was sweet and he was happy they had avoided the disease but seeing them how they were now saddened him to his very soul.

Looking at their ravaged remains, birds had quite obviously had their fill leaving only what he now saw which was something he certainly didn't want his companions to witness. It was bad enough that he now had these images to remember, he would at least spare Naomi and

Shaznay the same fate as heard them call from behind him. He instantly told them all was ok but to stay put until he said otherwise, this giving him at least chance to remove the sad sight that he knew would remain stuck in his mind for the rest of his life. He glanced around the small deck grabbing a large tarp that lay towards the front of the boat. Frank slowly used what energy he had left to lift and drop the remains individually into the water, ensuring it was on the opposite side to where his friends remained bobbing on the cold, choppy tide. During his task, the stench of death had made him wretch but he knew despite his disgust and discomfort in performing the job it was the right thing and a necessity for him to do.

As he wiped some blood from his hands and looked out onto the water, to his relief the tide seemed to carry the two bodies down towards the deep and in a different direction to his friends leaving him the chance to sigh heavily and rest for a minute after what he had just had to do. Finally walking over to his companions he unclipped the ladder and lowered it down for them to climb aboard, taking the weapons and petrol from them in the process still breathing heavily from the exertions of his previous task. He knew he couldn't dwell on it though, they had made it this far now, he just hoped the two bodies had become stranded due to a simple lack of fuel rather than some form of mechanical fault on the craft. He hardly fancied the swim back to the beach should the boat be broken. He knew as the two women worriedly looked at the blood stained deck that it was time for him to find out their fate.

It wasn't the fastest of things but so far it was doing what they needed as the small boat bounced off one of the larger waves, the spray of saltwater covering every inch of the deck and those who stood on it. Shaznay had the controls and seemed to be having the time of her life while the other two ate in peace for once not having to watch their backs for the flesh hungry freaks that would normally be lurking everywhere. It felt strange as they weren't usually given a second to complete such a simple task, constantly having to watch over their shoulders with everything that they did. Shaznay had jumped at the chance to take the controls as soon as the engine had grumbled its way to life, stating that she would eat once she had taken them all to safety. It seemed the belief and excitement within her was strong, hoping that something good would be waiting on the other side of the channel and who were the other two to argue with her. After all they had no idea what they would discover, they just hoped that she was indeed correct with her hopes and dreams as she continued smiling at the water that lay before her. They had no real idea in what direction they were going, simply using the notion that if they continued heading away from England they would eventually hit France. It was a pretty foolproof plan, which now gave them only one thing to do, simply relax and enjoy the fact that for the next few hours at least they would be free from zombies and perhaps heading towards a new, and hopefully virus free future.

Chapter 29

For the last hour the new land had been coming ever closer, they had almost reached France and the anticipation was close to killing the trio onboard the small boat which continued to chug its way towards the solid ground. Frank had taken over the controls while the two women stood on the deck watching intently, trying to spot anything that might give them a clue about what they would encounter upon docking. They were approaching what looked like some fenced off woodland which would certainly suffice as a landing point and if the distant view served them correctly the chain links had been breached in various places allowing easy access to the unknown country beyond. This was certainly in one sense a positive sight for the group, the barbed wire coils would have made the fence pretty un-climbable, they just hoped that the damage caused was not from the dead army that they were of course trying to leave well behind. They doubted it though, the damaged areas seemed the work of at least a little skill and after all these things were definitely not mentally or physically equipped to cut holes or perform any sort of complex task like this one.

As they continued on, their boat moving as fast as it would there had been thankfully no signs of the creatures that they had noticed. As a strong breeze hit them, Naomi walked over to Frank enquiring as to whether she should shout for attention. He hesitated for a moment before telling Shaznay to ease off on the throttle, allowing the boat to slow gradually on the tide. He knew that she had made a good point and that perhaps rushing in could be a fatal mistake, this was after all unknown territory for them all. Should there be hoards of zombies lying in wait it would certainly be better to alert the bastards while they were safe and out of reach on the water rather than presenting themselves as a ready served meal on the land ahead. It was after all possible that the wooded area could be teeming with the bastards which was something he had not yet given enough thought to.

The three of them stood stationary looking into the trees that lay only quarter of a mile ahead as the pressing wind hit them from the side causing Shaznay to hold onto Frank in a simple effort to shield herself from the cold intrusion. Frank looked down at her huddled form and smiled before cupping one hand to his mouth and bellowing "hello" so loudly that it hurt his throat. His deep voice seemed to echo over the wind as they looked on in anticipation waiting anxiously for any sign of movement or life hoping that they had found the uninfected paradise that they so longed for. As seconds passed that seemed like hours nothing happened, no one responded, no people or zombies emerged, the branches of the many trees continued to bounce in the breeze as they looked on at this possible Eden in hope.

They waited for well over a minute before Naomi finally shouted again, repeating the same greeting as loud as she could in yet another attempt to rouse some form of life from the country that they had reached. Once again they received no reply, looking at each other silently, each wondering if it was indeed time to simply dock and hope for the best. Without verbally agreeing they each nodded in silence, their previous excitement and hope being replaced with a fear now as they accepted nervously what they were about to do. It was time to find out what awaited ahead.

They faced no choice but to get their legs wet as they clambered into the water, Frank grasping one of the ropes in order to stop the boat from drifting away on the current. About twenty yards from the shore he faced a struggle as he told the girls to keep an eye out for any movement ahead, his concerns spread between the possibility of attack and their means of escape should they need one. With every laboured and energy sapping step he edged closer to the fence. He hoped that the rope would stretch far enough and that the boat wouldn't become grounded in the shallow water, the last thing he wanted was to become stranded. As he took another step a scream erupted from ahead, the sound causing him instantly to tense as his footing slipped on a rock beneath the surface. Before he even had chance to look up he became submerged in the shallow water, the rope slipping from his grasp as he struggled to get back to his standing position. Panic hit him as his head rose from the surface, he had known the scream had come from one of the girls as he gathered his bearings seeing the boat drifting slowly away first before spinning a hundred and eighty degrees to see exactly what he had feared. Gunshots rang out as he saw Naomi and Shaznay firing into the oncoming hoard of creatures, the bullets felling some of them momentarily however more followed from within the heavily wooded area.

Unarmed, Frank knew he had to reach the boat, looking at the army ahead it would be the only form of escape for them as he began to swim as fast as his tired body would allow. He hurt everywhere, tired from all the exertions he tried to move as fast as possible noticing pretty quickly that he faced a task that was simply too much for him to accomplish. With every laboured stroke he took the boat seemed to move twice as far, his kicks in the water no match for the current and side wind that carried away his hopes of surviving this new found mess. It was as he gave up his chase and began to tread water that he heard another female scream from behind him, the sound causing his heart to stop as he turned towards the shriek. "Hang on." Were the words that escaped his mouth as once again he began kicking furiously this time knowing that if he didn't move fast enough it would cost Shaznay her life.

Naomi and Shaznay had become separated by about ten metres, their constant attempts of dodging and fighting the zombies meaning their movements had not been coordinated. Shaznay now lay on her back, two of the creatures having reached her, now snapping their jaws in a bid to taste her warm flesh as she fought with everything she could against the infected figures of which she knew there were more to follow. Naomi was trying her hardest to help, at least ten of the things now separating them along with however many would emerge from the trees in the meantime as she furiously tried to change the mag of her rifle, giving up in the process and retrieving her magnum instead. As she opened fire, instantly popping two zombie heads she saw Frank emerge from the water to her left. She realized thankfully that he would reach Shaznay before she ever could, hopefully in time to save her as she watched him sprint to her aid on his exhausted legs. It was as the gun was knocked from Shaznay's grasp that Frank threw a kick at the first attacker, the rotting corpse falling to its side with a crunch as its rib cage almost disintegrated from the vicious blow. Shaznay managed to push the second zombie from the mounted position above her and scramble to her feet, retrieving her fallen weapon at the same time. She pointed the automatic at her second attacker and pressed the trigger, happily emptying three bullets into the monsters face before spitting on its motionless figure.

As she grinned at her rescue and looked up towards the man that had saved her life she heard him grunt as he fell backwards towards the sand. Before she even had time to react it was too late for her to return the favour that he had just done for her. So engrossed in helping Shaznay he had never seen the three creatures emerge from the woodland, slowly heading towards the trio unnoticed amongst the chaos. It had been these three cadavers that simultaneously pulled Frank to the ground and it was these corpses that now took his life, Shaznay only capable of watching on in horror. Powerless to react the first bite had been fatal, tearing through the side of his neck and severing his jugular, he had been unable to fire a shot or throw a punch before consciousness had almost immediately slipped away from him. By the time Shaznay had managed to scream and begun firing into the crowd he had been on the verge of death, his motionless blood soaked body unaware of everything around him. Her rescue attempt was useless as she shot the attackers individually before kneeling next to his stricken figure, cradling his limp head on her legs as the tears began to flow, her legs soon becoming drenched in his warm crimson blood. She knew through her sobs that he was dead, the sheer amount of blood that covered everything around telling her everything she needed to know as she kissed his forehead. With hardly any time to accept what had happed with shots and groans ringing in her ears she felt a hand on her should causing her to gasp and roll away in fear of being taken herself.

"It's me, it's me!" Were the words that followed as she looked through her teary eyes to see Naomi standing above her, with a raised hand which when accepted helped her back to her feet. "I am so sorry babe, I really am but you know we have to move." She continued, Shaznay sobbing once again but nodding at the same time in agreement as she stooped down, retrieved Frank's gear and placed one last kiss on his face. Once again despite the fact that she just wanted to curl up and give in she simply couldn't, they were unable to stop for even the shortest time grief stricken or not. Through her tiredness and tears, facing no choice but to leave Frank's body behind she once again began to run for her life hoping and praying that they would stumble on safety or rescue. With the many groans now filling the air it seemed very doubtful.

Chapter 30

With laboured breath they could only stare at this spectacle of hope before them. What looked like a makeshift army barracks lay waiting about five hundred yards ahead of them. Since the devastating loss of Frank, they had been running nonstop for the best part of an hour, using more energy than they should have possibly possessed to avoid the swarms of zombies that just like England lined every street and pavement around them. On their first impressions of this new country they had been certain that the plague had taken everything, the signs of despair and death proof that they would never find rescue, their battle seemingly destined to be never-ending. Suddenly though, only moments ago these thoughts had dramatically changed as they had rounded a corner only to be greeted by the camouflaged, gun mounted barrier and what looked like an athletics stadium beyond housing all kinds of army tents and vehicles. It was this that they still stared at, transfixed, walking one pace at a time in silence knowing that there was little to be said, both hoping that they had discovered what could be their salvation.

Controlled by a simple laptop and located at a safe enough distance a hundred yards from behind the barrier Georges St Claire sat looking through the scope of a Gatling gun. He had been the first to notice the two female figures come into view as he had been sat watching the same repetitive zombie filled screen that he did every day. His only job to simply open fire and obliterate any of the rotting bastards that stumbled their way too close to camp. With this newest arrival, he had been unsure at first but the more he had looked the more he had been positive that the two women were actually uninfected humans. Not only that, they were the first living people that he had seen outside the camp in months. After screaming for his colleagues, he had now been joined by several of them at the laptop including his senior Captain Raif Parker, who when needed would issue any instruction on how to move forward with the current situation. For now though, the on looking men and women simply watched and examined, trying to spot any sign or hint of infection before they even attempted contact with these two new figures. They knew from all that they had seen that the disease could be carried for quite some time before the change actually took place meaning that the up most caution would be taken at all times.

Seeing what they now saw and actually contemplating contact rather than destroying anything that moved was certainly a new experience for all of the soldiers within the quarters. So far through this hell they had simply survived by allowing no one into or even close to the barracks, which had initially been set up as a training camp for the American and French soldiers that still remained within the confines. Luckily part of that training had included ammunition and weaponry, which was the main reason behind their survival and success since the zombie mayhem had begun. The actions that they had taken in order to avoid the contaminated had been harsh ones, each soldier accepting that they had killed many innocents in the first days of the infection spreading. They had faced no other choice though ensuring above all with the perimeter guns that they simply weren't penetrated and that they remained as far away from being bitten as possible. Had they been instructed to, they would have tried to help but there had been no such orders or commands from either the French or American superiors. There had been only silence, which had left them stranded and glued to the spot amongst the ever-increasing hell. So far though, their methods of survival had been flawless.

The lack of radio contact from anyone outside their small camp did not fill them with much hope though, anyone else's survival and the outlook for the future seemingly bleak as they found it impossible to contact anyone from the outside world.

There were only twenty-four people within the borders of their barracks and it had until moments ago seemed that they were perhaps the last people alive. Now though things had changed as the two figures edged ever closer to one of the loaded and deadly weapons that had taken so many lives already.

They were within two hundred yards of their target when it struck, their gaze was so fixated on the possible safety ahead that they had become careless. Their focus and concentration centred on the possibility of rescue rather than the creatures around which was a mistake that they suddenly began to regret as Shaznay let out a scream.

The clammy grip she felt on the back of her neck making her heart sink instantly as she horrifyingly realised what was happening. The zombie had crept out from a small side street, the naked and rotting cadaver moving silently thanks to the fact it had no throat from which it could groan, allowing it to approach the two women completely unannounced. Within the blink of an eye it had grasped the back of Shaznay pulling her off balance, sending them both crashing to the tarmac with a thud. Her weapon skidded away across the ground leaving her only with her hands and feet as a form of defence as she began to fight underneath the deadly creature that seemed to have her pinned. As she struggled to thrust her hand upwards in an attempted punch three things happened almost simultaneously. Shaznay was bitten, the zombie was grounded and the roar of gunfire echoed around the city streets.

Shaznay's badly aimed shot to the zombies jaw had missed by mere inches presenting her bare flesh directly in front of the monster's face. As it clamped down on the meat it craved, blood was drawn instantly leaving Shaznay struggling to accept the sudden fate that she had been left with. As Naomi screamed helplessly at the scene below and fired a shot into the skull of the attacker she realised her reaction to the incident had been a moment too late. Tears began to flow as she watched the creature topple to the ground as Shaznay angrily clutched at her arm whilst scrambling back to her feet.

It was as the soldiers watched the now infected woman rise to a standing position once again on the small laptop screen that Georges heard the simple order from his Captain.

"Target's are compromised, open fire."

Naomi saw the orange flash out of the corner of her eye before Shaznay's face seemed to explode in a moment that seemed so surreal as she watched on in complete horror. She felt the warm blood and gore spatter her own skin as her thoughts shot into confusion, her mind struggling to find an explanation as to what was happening less than a foot away from her. The roar of gunfire invaded her senses as Shaznay's body began to fall in what seemed like slow motion, all the while bullets tearing her to pieces although the first shot had seen to the fact that she was most certainly dead.

It was just as Naomi's terrified mind slotted together the pieces of this sudden puzzle that the chain of bullets moved across to her. She felt a white-hot pain as the first few entered at chest level, pulverizing her rib cage and lungs but the pain was short lived. It took less than two seconds from her witnessing the obliteration of Shanay's face to the simple nothingness that now took over as her own skull was shredded by the powerful weapon that continued to hurl forward its deadly projectiles. Before the racket of gunfire stopped, both Naomi and Shaznay's remains lay still on the concrete, destined to rot like all those that they had been trying so hard to avoid. Their journey it seemed was finally over.

It was with a heavy heart and a saddened sigh that he had entered the four-digit combination and pressed enter with a slightly shaking finger. Almost instantly the Gatling gun had erupted spewing forward its deadly contents at a frightening rate, the two figures that had come within touching distance of the barracks simply torn to shreds by the ten seconds of shattering gunfire that they had been powerless to avoid.

As Georges now looked at the unmoving remains and slowly shook his head now that the deafening sounds had stopped, the screen that he looked at asked if a repeat procedure was needed. He knew that it was certainly not; for them to have survived it was a simple impossibility.

They would have been dead before they had even heard the gunfire and he knew it. Just like the plague around them, nothing survived such devastation and he knew that eventually, even despite the awesome arsenal that they had within the camp this constant plague of death would catch up with them too. After all despite the fact there were two dozen of them, they did not have an eternal supply of food or ammunition leaving them the knowledge that they couldn't stay put forever and also with one simple fact to accept. Whereas their ammo would eventually diminish, the dead army would simply keep on coming. The plague would reach them of that Georges was sure as he wiped away a solitary tear at what he had just done. He knew it was simply a matter of time.

"Hell is the place where one has ceased to hope."
A.J. Cronin

1665041R0011

Printed in Great Britain
by Amazon.co.uk, Ltd.,
Marston Gate.